The last thing Waco expected was to become a deputy marshal. Yet he found himself wearing a badge. He soon learned there was more to being a lawman than walking the streets, making arrests and pocketing a share of the fines. Speed with a gun was needed and he had it. But there was more. He needed to be a detective, a diplomat, sometimes ruthless, occasionally sympathetic.

Guided by the Rio Hondo gun wizard, Dusty Fog, Waco learned fast and well. Then came his greatest test. The girl he loved was held captive by a ruthless outlaw and could not be saved without endangering innocent lives.

That was when Waco finally learned just what it took to make a lawman.

Books by J. T. EDSON
Arranged in chronological order of stories

† In preparation   ★Awaiting publication
and published by Corgi Books

THE MAKING
OF A LAWMAN

CORGI BOOKS
A DIVISION OF TRANSWORLD PUBLISHERS LTD
A NATIONAL GENERAL COMPANY

THE MAKING OF A LAWMAN

A CORGI BOOK 552 093491

First publication in Great Britain

PRINTING HISTORY
Corgi edition published 1968
Corgi edition reissued 1973

Copyright © J. T. Edson 1968

This book is set in 9-10½ pt. Plantin

Corgi Books are published by Transworld Publishers Ltd.,
Cavendish House, 57-59 Uxbridge Road,
Ealing, London, W.5.
Made and printed in Great Britain by
Hunt Barnard Printing Ltd., Aylesbury, Bucks.

NOTE: The Australian price appearing on the back
cover is the recommended retail price.

For Mike Legat,
who agreed to try my
Rockabye County stories

Author's note: While complete in itself, the events in this book run concurrently with those in THE TROUBLE BUSTERS.

I

A Special Kind of Man

"To all this I swear, so help me God," said the boy whose only name was Waco, completing the oath which made him a deputy town marshal of Mulrooney, Kansas.

While pinning the badge to his black and white calf-skin vest, the youngster could hardly hold down a faint, unbelieving grin. Six, or even three, months ago the suggestion that he might become a peace officer would have been met with derision. Yet there he stood, faced by Mulrooney's mayor and town marshal, a member of the civic law enforcement body.

Just over six foot in height, with a frame developing to its full power, Waco dressed and looked what he was, a Texas cowhand. His black J.B. Stetson hat, distinctively shaped, gave as clear an indication of his place of birth as did the star motif carved on his high-heeled boots. The hat hung on a peg by the door, exposing his curly blond hair to view. Tanned by the elements, his handsome face had strength, although the blue eyes no longer bore a wolf-cautious glint and his mouth smiled more easily than previously. Tight-rolled and knotted about his throat, the scarlet bandana trailed long ends over a blue shirt almost to the waistband of the levis pants. The gunbelt around his middle had been tooled to his fit and carried a pair of staghorn-handled 1860 Army Colts in holsters designed for speed on the draw. Something in the way he wore the rig warned it was no mere affectation.

Looking at Waco, Mayor Woods felt a momentary doubt at his suitability for the post. The town was one of those which had grown up along the trans-continental railroad, hoping to gain its livelihood from the almost numberless longhorn cattle brought north in search of a market. Being Mulrooney's leading citizen and partially responsible for its conception, the mayor wanted it to prosper. In which case the correct kind of law enforcement would be essential.

Could a boy not yet eighteen give the type of service required? Only the previous day Mayor Woods had seen Waco draw his right hand Colt with blinding speed and kill a man trying to shoot a friend. Yet, inexperienced in such matters, the mayor realised that being an efficient peace officer called for more than a fast draw and accurate shooting. True some trail-end towns asked no more of their marshals than gun-skill, but Mayor Woods thought that to be a short-sighted policy and not what Mulrooney required.

The worry over the age side of the matter might also apply to another of the three deputies—and even to the man Mayor Woods had selected to be the town's first marshal.

Almost as tall as Waco, and lean as a steer reared in the greasewood country, the Ysabel Kid seemed even younger. At first glance the sight of his handsome, almost babyishly innocent face, the all black clothing, walnut-handled Dragoon Colt buttforward in the low cavalry draw holster at the right side of his belt and ivory-hilted James Black bowie knife sheathed on its left, might tend to raise a mocking smile. Then one noticed the Indian-dark features, red hazel eyes and rapidly reached the conclusion that here stood no mere dressed-up boy trying to pose as a tough, mean man. Young he might be, but the years had been spent learning hard lessons that had prepared him well for the future. However, he too failed to comply with the popular conception of a trail-end town lawman.

While the third deputy certainly seemed fitted for the part, it was a specialised one. Big Sarah Shelley wore a plain gingham dress instead of the garish costume she used when serving behind the bar of Mayor Woods' Fair Lady saloon. Red-headed, good-looking tall and buxom, although hard-fleshed and far from flabby, she looked ideally suited for her work as matron in charge of handling female prisoners.

If the two male deputies appeared an unusual selection, the man chosen by Mayor Woods to be marshal—chief law enforcement officer of the town—seemed, on the face of it, even more so.

At most he stood no more than five foot six, with dusty blond hair and a pleasantly good-looking face. Although dressed in expensive, well-made range clothes, he gave them the appearance of being somebody's cheap cast-offs. Nor did the excellently made gunbelt, with matched, white-handled Army Colts in its two cross draw holsters, greatly add to his stature or notice-ability. All in all, at first glance, he looked like an insignificant nobody. Closer inspection revealed that his face had strength of will and intelligence, while his lack of inches failed to prevent him from possessing the muscular development of a Hercules.

During the Civil War, as a seventeen-year old Confederate States cavalry captain, that small, insignificant cowhand built a reputation equalled only by the great Turner Ashby and John Singleton Mosby; although he gained it on the less-publicised Arkansas battle-front. After the War ended he had been called from his work as segundo of the biggest ranch in Texas and sent into Mexico on a dangerous, exceedingly delicate mission which he had carried out successfully.* Since then his name had gone out as a cowhand of the first water, trail boss second to none, the lawman who tamed a wild Montana gold town after three less able officers had died trying.† Texans boasted of his uncanny bare-hand fighting skill which rendered bigger men helpless; or told about his wizardry in the matter of rapid draw-ing and straight shooting with his two long barrelled Army Colts.

Small he might be, but nobody ever thought of Dusty Fog in a matter of mere feet and inches. In reputation or actual deeds he stood as tall as any man.

In addition to acting as the OD Connected's segundo, Dusty also rode with its floating outfit. On the large spreads of the great open-range grazing days, a group of six or so cowhands were employed to work the extremities of a ranch. Accom-panied by a chuck wagon, or taking food along on mule-back, they acted as a mobile ranch crew. During his trip into Mexico, Dusty had met and hired the Ysabel Kid and Mark Counter to form the nucleus of the OD Connected's floating outfit. How-ever, the general state of unrest in Texas caused them to spend more time trouble-shooting in various places than riding their ranch's ranges.

Bringing the OD Connected herd north, Dusty heard rumours of the two new towns and saw one or the other would shorten his drive. So he and the Kid headed for Brownton while Waco and the fourth member of the floating outfit came into

*Told in THE YSABEL KID.
†Told in QUIET TOWN.

9

Mulrooney.* From what Dusty saw, Brownton was no place to take his herd. Despite the fact that Mark Counter had received a wound in the Fair Lady Saloon, Dusty concluded that Mulrooney offered his trail crew a fairer deal than its rival metropolis. His decision struck Mayor Woods almost as a god-sent gift. Being fresh from the East, none of the citizens knew enough to handle the law. In the mayor's opinion, Dusty Fog ideally filled her needs. Especially with the backing of his friends.

Take the Ysabel Kid as a start. There stood a man whom any honest peace officer would count fortunate to have at his side.

Not that such had always been the case. Until meeting Dusty that day on the Brownsville trail, the Kid had been regarded as something of a one-boy crime wave; a border-smuggler with one foot on the slippery slope that led to real law-busting. The meeting changed all that and now the Kid's early upbringing made him a most useful member of range-country society.

Born the only son of a wild Irish-Kentuckian and his French Creole-Comanche wife, the Kid spent his boyhood living as a member of the *Pehnane* band of his mother's tribe. There he learned all those things a brave-heart warrior needed to know†, skill with weapons, ability to read sign or discover hidden enemies, horse-savvy of a high degree. Fortunately for the peace of Texas he never found the need to use his training while among the *Pehnane*, although it came in handy at various times in later years. Maybe the Kid did not rate high as a gun-fighter, being only fair with his Dragoon Colt, but he claimed few peers in the matter of handling a knife or a rifle.

Like the Kid, Waco was a product of the times. Left an orphan in a Waco Indian attack on a wagon train, he grew up among the large family of an impoverished rancher. Although treated as one of the family, some urge set him drifting at the age of thirteen. Even then he carried a gun, a battered but operational old Navy Colt. Four years later he wore a brace of Army Colts and bore a log-sized chip on his shoulder. Working for Clay Allison's wild onion crew had given him truculence and might have sent him on the trail of Wes Hardin, Bad Bill Longley or other fast-handed *Tejano* boys running from the law after a killing too many.

*Told in THE TROUBLE BUSTERS.
†Told in COMANCHE.

Then fate stepped in. Waco met Dusty Fog, the fastest of them all. From the time that Dusty saved the youngster's life, hauling him clear when a stampeding herd threatened to run him down, Waco became a changed person.* With Clay Allison's blessing, Waco quit the CA and rode north as a member of the OD Connected. During the last weeks of the drive a change in him had become apparent. No longer did he regard all men as potential enemies. He smiled easier, took part in night camp horse-play. Sure he still wore his guns, but under Dusty's tuition he restrained his eagerness to use them.

All in all Dusty felt satisfied that he could run the law. He knew Texans, could handle them and figured he could deal with the railroad workers, buffalo-hunters or others who would also use the town. Mayor Woods and the Town Council gave him a free hand, promised no interference with his methods. Backed by the Kid, Waco, Big Sarah and Mark, when the latter recovered from his wound, he reckoned that he could make Mulrooney a decent town and one in which everybody received a fair deal. In that desire he had the blessing of the mayor.

While there might possibly be other female mayors in the United States, it was unlikely that any of them equalled Freddie Woods in the matter of beauty. Five foot eight in height, with raven black hair topping a regally beautiful face, she would turn heads in any crowd. The sober, if expensive, black suit and white blouse she wore for performing a civic function set off a truly magnificent figure with rich mature curves. The fact that she ran a saloon did nothing to detract from her acceptance by the most influential people in town. Everybody knew the British aristocracy had eccentric ways and Freddie Woods had been born the Right Honourable Winifred Amelia Besgrave-Woodstole. Why the rich, talented, beautiful daughter of an English lord had come to the United States and wound up running a saloon in a trail-end town has been told elsewhere. She came, gained election as mayor and now worked to give the voters satisfaction.

With the oath-taking ceremony over, Freddie looked at the young faces before her.

"I'm not going to make a speech," she said. "Just do what you're hired for and we'll be satisfied."

"We'll do just that," Dusty promised. "Lon, you'd best—."

*Told in TRIGGER FAST.

11

Hooves thundered along the street outside the office, punctuated by ringing cowhand whoops, screeches and shots.

"Could be this's where we start to earn our pay," the Kid commented, crossing to the window and looking out.

Much what he expected to see greeted the Kid's gaze. Galloping along came a trio of trail-dirty, unshaven young cowhands. None of them belonged to the OD Connected, which had paid off the previous night and had given the citizens of Mulrooney an idea of what celebrating trail-drivers meant. While raising a considerable ruckus, the trio did not endanger other lives, but kept to the centre of the street and sent their bullets straight up into the air. Heading for the Fair Lady Saloon, they saw the marshal's office building and brought their horses to a halt.

"Yeeah!" whooped the tallest of the three, a well-made, good looking youngster. "Let's smoke the John Law's hole some."

With that he threw a shot at the building. Glass shattered as the bullet struck a window. It was a most satisfactory sound, one which delighted the trio and stirred up the desire to hear more. Restraining their fiddle-footing horses, they tossed more lead at the building. Not all of it hit the windows, but enough struck home to increase their delight.

Catching Freddie around the waist, Dusty swept her down behind the desk. At the same moment Big Sarah dived through the open door leading to the cells in the rear of the building. Out flashed Waco's Colts and he started for the door, ready to do battle.

"Hold it, boy!" Dusty barked.

Reluctantly, showing his surprise, Waco skidded to a halt by the door. The building's walls had been constructed strongly enough to stop revolver bullets and he flattened himself to the right of the door as lead drove into the thick timber. Despite the anger he felt, he stood still and waited for further orders.

"You fixing to let 'em get away with this, Dusty?" Waco demanded.

"Well no, I don't reckon I am," Dusty replied with a smile. "Only I don't want to shoot them either."

"Would you mind getting off my chest, Captain Fog?" Freddie put in a mite breathlessly, still on the floor with the small Texan holding her down.

"I thought you'd never ask," he replied and started to rise.

Derisive howls and yells rose from the three cowhands. Then,

12

having failed to produce the local law, they tired of the pastime and headed for the Fair Lady at a wild gallop. Bringing their horses to a halt, they tossed reins across the hitching rail and tramped into the building.

"What the he—," Waco began, then rephrased his words for Freddie's benefit. "What're you figuring on doing about them yahoos, Dusty?"

"Go along and remonstrate with 'em," Dusty replied.

"I'd toss 'em in the pokey!" yelped Big Sarah indignantly, emerging from the rear. "To hell with that there remon— whatever you said."

"We'll let Dusty try it his way first," smiled Freddie. "Mind if I come along to watch?"

"Come ahead," Dusty replied and walked towards the front door.

At that hour of the morning, the Fair Lady had not yet opened for business. Only the fact that the swamper did his work inside caused the doors to be unlocked. Behind the bar, Donna—another of the girls who tended to the customers' needs—checked on stock ready for the day's trade. Neither she nor the swamper, a grizzled old timer, showed any great pleasure at the trio's arrival.

"We're not open yet, boys," Donna warned.

"Let's have some glasses then, ma'am," the tallest cowhand replied. "Monte, you go fetch that bottle that's done kept us warm and comfy all the way in."

"I surely will, Tack," answered the shortest, who sported an early attempt at moustache-growing. "Boy oh boy, we sure showed that marshal that we'd come to town."

"That we did," enthused the third member of the trio. "He never even showed his lil Kansas head outside at-all."

Leaving to collect the bottle of cheap whiskey from Tack's saddle pouch, Monte returned with it and news.

"The marshal's done coming," he told his delighted companions.

"We'll have him buy us a drink, Brother Tack," grinned the third youngster.

"Sure will, Brother Del," agreed Tack. "Why 'twouldn't be fitting for him not to set them up for some of Colonel Charlie's boys."

"We'ns ride for Colonel Charlie Goodnight, ma'am," Del

13

told Donna with an air of pride and superiority.

"I bet he lies awake at night praying that his good luck lasts," the buxom blonde answered and waited expectantly for the arrival of the town's newly-elected marshal.

If the trio felt any concern at the approach of the marshal, they failed to show it. Having just completed their first drive, they wished to give the impression of being well-travelled veterans. Fed on highly-spiced accounts of how a trail crew acted when in town, they had come into Mulrooney as they believed would be expected of them. Already, in their opinions, they had made a good start by asserting their Texas superiority over the Kansas lawmen. All that remained for them to do was buckle down and show those Kansan grasshoppers how Colonel Charlie's crew whooped up a storm on hitting town.

Leaning with their backs to the bar, the trio watched the bat-wing doors swing open. On the way to town they had drunk enough to dull their perceptions. So they failed to take in the significant signs which ought to have spelled danger to range-wise minds.

"It's the law, Brother Tack," announced Del, standing at the right of the group.

"Naw," corrected Monte from the left. "It's the marshal's lil son playing at sheriffs 'n' owlhoots. Don't he look the fiercest thing that ever growed?"

"Trouble being that he stopped growing a whole heap too soon," Tack answered, setting down the whiskey bottle on the bar. "Hey, bar-lady, is this here half-portion the best your town can afford in the shape of a lawman?"

Standing with the other deputies and Freddie outside the bat-wing doors, the Kid raised his eyes to heaven as if searching for strength.

"Lordy lord!" he breathed. "I allus figured cowhands didn't have a lick of good sense. But these three're plumb foolish."

"They'll likely learn," Waco growled, deeply annoyed and bristling at the insults to his hero.

"And soon," guessed Big Sarah.

Freddie remained silent, watching Dusty and wondering how he intended to handle the matter. Running the law in a trail-end town took a special kind of man. Unless Freddie missed her guess, the next few minutes would prove whether Dusty had the necessary qualifications.

14

While advancing to the bar, Dusty studied the cowhands and assessed the situation. Leading men since his sixteenth birthday had given him the ability to read them and gauge their potential. Everything he saw told him that gun-play would not be needed. None of the trio looked that kind of proddy. Sure they all wore guns, a Texan who did not being something of a rarity, but none showed signs of coming close to his own standard. However they needed firm handling, as a warning to themselves and others that the law could not be flouted in Mulrooney.

If the cowhands had consulted with him previously they could hardly have stood more suitably for Dusty's needs. Almost shoulder to shoulder they lined the bar and eyed him with tolerant contempt. Then they learned the error of their ways.

As a boy, possibly to divert attention from his small size, Dusty had developed and improved a natural tendency to being ambidextrous. The ability to use either hand for every purpose often came in useful—and did at that moment.

Suddenly, giving no hint of what he aimed to do, Dusty drove up both his hands, arcing them outwards. With the speed and co-ordination that enabled him to draw and shoot in under a second, he crashed a back-hand blow into Monte and Del's jaws. He hit with such force and so unexpectedly that the two cowhands spun away from Tack along the bar.

Even as realisation knifed into Tack, he found troubles of his own. Down swung Dusty's left fist and rammed with considerable force into the cowhand's belly. While Tack might be as tough as working ten to eighteen hours a day could make him, he still felt the punch. Pain doubled him over and the air belched from his lungs in a rush.

Nor had Dusty finished. Catching Tack by the rear of the collar and seat of the pants, he heaved the youngster at Del with enough force to tumble them in a tangled heap to the floor. Monte started forward, hands reaching out at Dusty and a desire for revenge in his heart. Swivelling around fast, Dusty clamped his two hands around Monte's right wrist. Then, carrying the trapped arm into the air, Dusty pivoted underneath it and snapped it down. Letting out a bewildered wail, Monte felt his feet leave the ground. For a moment it seemed that the room spun around and he lit down upon the sprawling bodies of his companions.

For a moment the trio lay winded and dazed. Finally they

15

rolled apart and sat up to stare about them. Only they no longer looked at a small, insignificant man. In some manner Dusty seemed to have put on height and heft until he stood taller than any of them. Monte expressed his companions' feelings.

"Hey!" he yelped in an aggrieved tone. "Where'd the lil feller go?"

2

Cowhands are Only Part Of It

"On your feet!" Dusty snapped and the trio obeyed with considerable speed.

"What're you fixing to do with us, marshal?" Tack asked worriedly.

"Take you to jail for whooping up the town and damned near shooting the mayor."

Instead of distressing the trio, the latter piece of information seemed to amuse them. Broad grins creased their faces.

"We-all did that?" gurgled Monte, slapping a hand against his thigh. "Ain't that a pistol. We'ns near on done shot their mayor."

"And I didn't find it amusing!" interrupted a cold feminine voice.

So engrossed in staring at Dusty had the trio become, and delighted that they had given their companions at the herd such a good lead in the matter of hoorawing the town, that they failed to notice the batwing doors opening. Followed by the three deputies, Freddie stalked across the room. The cowhands turned, eyes raking Freddie from head to foot with frank juvenile admiration. Tack found his voice first, jerking off his hat.

"I sure bet the mayor didn't neither, ma'am," he said.

"I am the mayor!" Freddie replied.

Slowly the grins faded as the import of the words sank in. Three pairs of worried eyes darted from Freddie to Dusty, seeking confirmation of the remarkable statement and hoping to

16

see denial instead. While the rest of the trail hands would regard scaring a male mayor as a piece of good-natured fun, the same did not apply when that civic dignitary was a woman.

"Are you the for-real, sure-enough female lady mayor of this here town, ma'am?" gulped Del.

"I'm the for-real, sure-enough female lady mayor of this town," Freddie confirmed. "And I don't take to having lead whistling around my ears."

"Ma'am," said Monte fervently as he made a belated removal of his hat. "We didn't know you was in there."

"If we had," Del went on, "why we wouldn't've thought of shooting that ways, ma'am."

"You should've thought on it afore you started," Dusty growled. "Let's head for the pokey."

"We'ns work for Colonel Charlie Goodnight," Tack pointed out.

"Which same he's just going to fall on your necks with whoops of joy when he hears what you've been doing," Dusty drawled.

"You-all don't know Colonel Charlie, happen that's what you reckon," Del put in, an uneasy feeling forming that his employer would not regard the trio's behaviour as commendable.

"Reckon I don't know him?" Dusty smiled. "I rode with him on that third drive he made to Fort Sumner after the War."

"You was on that drive?" Tack asked, with less disbelief than he might have shown earlier.

"On it!" the Kid put in. "Boy, he was Colonel Charlie's segundo."

Which explained a whole lot more to the Texans than it did to Freddie. All three knew the name of Goodnight's segundo on that fateful third drive to Fort Sumner, a journey which helped pave the way for the longer trails north to the Kansas market.

"Lordy lord!" Del breathed, admiration glowing in his eyes. "You're Dusty Fog. No wonder you licked us so easy."

"What's going to happen to us, Cap'n Fog?" Tack inquired respectfully.

"I told you, you're going to the pokey. There're two windows bust—."

"Ole Tack here's the bestest window fixer in Medina County, Cap'n," Del began hopefully. "He could fit in new glass—."

"Who pays for it?" Dusty interrupted.

17

"Well now," Tack answered, hesitantly feeling into his pockets. "I'm bust."

"Me too," Del groaned.

"I ain't got but three dollars, 'cepting what the boys gave me to bring back the makings and stuff for them," Monte went on.

"I'll tell you what," Freddie remarked, recalling something Dusty had told her about cowhands the previous day. "The backhouse hole needs to go down deeper. If you three put it down, I'll pay for the windows and Tack can fix them."

"Dig?" yelped Del.

"I ain't never took to working on the blister end of a shovel, ma'am," Monte went on.

"Then you can wait in a cell until I've seen Uncle Charlie and asked for your fine money," Dusty told them, inwardly grinning at the way Freddie handed out a punishment.

"Can't say as how I'm took with that idea either," Monte groaned. "You're sure enough kin to Colonel Charlie. That kind of meanness goes in families, they do reckon."

Watching the trio's expressions, Freddie found increasing difficulty in maintaining her coldly regal pose. She could read the growing realisation that a trap had closed around them. All three knew just how Goodnight would regard finding them in jail. They could also visualise their companions' reactions to hearing what had caused the delay in the arrival of much-needed supplies of tobacco and the like. Despite a cowhand's antipathy to handling a shovel, all three felt it better to dig than be held in jail.

"We'll do it," Tack decided. "Happen we work at it, we'll be done soon enough to get back to the herd in time for supper."

"Digging's thirsty work," Freddie smiled. "You boys had better take a drink before you start."

Grins creased three faces and Tack took up the bottle they had brought in with them. Just as he started to pour out the drinks, he recalled his manners.

"Maybe you'd have one along of us, ma'am?"

"Thank you," Freddie replied, accepting the offered glass and raising it towards her lips. Then she sniffed at it instead of drinking. "What's this?"

"Whiskey, ma'am," Del answered.

"Is it?"

18

"Sure is, ma'am. Done bought it off a feller who met us on the range."

Ignoring Del's comment, Freddie took the bottle's neck between the extreme tips of her forefinger and thumb.

"Dispose of this slush, Donna," she ordered. "Give these gentlemen some decent liquor."

Watched by the cowhands, Donna dropped the bottle into the trash bucket behind the bar. Then she took one of the saloon's stock and poured out the drinks. The cowhands drank appreciatively and forgot any objections to losing their bottle.

"Whooee!" Tack commented, setting down the empty glass. "What've we been drinking all our lives?"

"On likker like this I can dig that there hole with my two bare hands," Del continued. "Lead me to it, ma'am."

"Tell you what," Dusty remarked. "Lon here's riding out just now. Give him the money. He'll buy that stuff for your pards with the herd and take it to them."

If any Kansas lawman had offered such a suggestion, it would have been regarded with at least suspicion. However the cowhands knew they could trust Dusty Fog. So Monte handed over the money and a scrawled list of goods to the Kid. Then the three cowhands trooped off to begin working out their fines.

Watching them go, Dusty felt sure that he had handled things just right. Back at the herd after finishing their chores, the trio would pass the word of their treatment. Soon news would spread that the law in Mulrooney treated cowhands fairly. Most of the trouble in other Kansas trail-end towns came from the citizens and lawmen cheating or abusing the visitors. That was one thing Dusty aimed to prevent at all costs.

"You handled that really well, Dusty," Freddie complimented.

"So did you," he returned. "It won't always be this easy though. Cowhands are only a part of it."

"If they drink stuff like this regularly," Freddie said, waving a hand to the glass of whiskey Tack had offered her and which still stood on the bar, "I can see how they would get mean."

Picking up the glass, Dusty sniffed at it and pulled a wry face. "It's the real, genuine snake-head base-burner for sure."

"They must use twenty-rattle sidewinders' heads in it," the Kid went on after following Dusty's example.

"I never saw a rattlesnake with twenty rattles on its tail," Freddie began.

"That's 'cause you've never been to Texas, ma'am," Waco informed her. "Why we've rattlers there with—."

"I'll bet you have,' she interrupted, but in such a friendly manner that he neither took offence nor felt snubbed. "What I don't see is the connection between rattlesnakes' heads and the whiskey."

"They drop the heads in to give it a kick when they're brewing it," the Kid explained. "Makes that fire-water so fierce that I don't know how they keep it bottled up."

"It's lucky those bunch hadn't drunk more than a couple of snorts apiece," Dusty put in, looking worried. "Happen they had, they might've been some harder to handle."

"They can buy better stuff than this at any place in town," Freddie said.

"Only they're not buying it in town," Dusty replied. "Let's go. When those three've put the hole down deep enough, see they fix the windows at the office, Sarah."

"Sure, Cap'n," the woman answered. "Where'll you be?"

"Around and about somewheres. Lon's heading out to the OD Connected camp to see about spreading the word that Brownton's bad medicine."

"You don't have to do that for us, Dusty," Freddie remarked.

"I'm not doing it for you," he assured her. "Those yahoos in Brownton 're fixing to trim the trail crews to the bone. They've got a civic ordnance that says nobody who supported the Confederate States, which means any Texan whether he supported it or not, can tote a gun in their town. That'll mean the trail-hands who turn in their guns're unarmed in a town full of folks who aren't. Any cowhand who goes home with his teeth and two eyes in his head'll be lucky, because that's just about all he will take. So I figure word ought to go out to warn them what to expect. What they do after that is up to their trail boss."

"They won't be treated like that here," Freddie promised.

'If I thought they would,' Dusty answered. 'You'd still be looking for a marshal." Then he looked at his two male deputies. "Come on, we've got work to do."

"I just knowed you'd get around to saying that," Waco groaned, darting glances around the room. "Where-at's Babsy, ma'am?"

"Upstairs resting," Freddie replied, "being, as you Texans put it, plumb tuckered out from all the fussing last night."

Although the girl in question had come from England to act as Freddie's maid, she had proven adept at providing the kind of entertainment saloon audiences enjoyed. Blonde, vivacious, buxom in a small way, her spirited renderings of Cockney songs and dances added to the general festivities celebrating the arrival of the first herd to Mulrooney. Waco found her especially attractive, but hoped to meet her again under less crowded conditions. However it did not seem that she would be making an appearance and Dusty showed signs of wanting to be on his way.

"Tell Mark that we'll be in to see him later," the small Texan requested.

"I bet he's up there in that big soft bed snoring like ten razor-back hawgs," the Kid went on.

"Trust him to get shot when there's work to be done," Waco commented and followed the other two into the street.

"How'd you have handled it, Boy?" Dusty asked as they left the saloon.

"I dunno. Gone in with a gun in my hand, likely," the youngster replied.

"Which could've sparked off a shooting," Dusty told him. "Throwing down with a gun's only part of being a lawman. You'll get on better by learning how to handle people. Those three kids aren't bad, just happied up a mite—."

"They just hadn't drunk enough of that wild mare's milk to make them mean," the Kid interjected.

"That's for sure," Dusty agreed, but put aside his thoughts on the matter so as to continue making his point to Waco. "With kids like that you don't need a gun. Just show them who's running things, treat them fair, then you'll get no trouble."

"Not as long as they drink decent whiskey," the Kid continued. "Which they sure wouldn't't've been had they finished that bottle they bought."

"That's for sure," Dusty admitted.

"Mind that time over to Newton when a feller was peddling snake-head gut-rot to the trail hands outside town?" the Kid went on.

"I'll never forget it," Dusty replied.

"What happened?" asked Waco.

"This jasper got a smart notion for making money. He stocked up with cheap whiskey and took a wagon on to the range. Used to peddle it to the trail-hands. Up that close to the

21

sale-pens they figured they could loosen off a mite and bought a couple of bottles. Only some of the hands got a mite too loose. After belting the bottles, a couple of them started grandstanding a mite reckless for some Eastern folks who'd come out to see a real, genuine trail herd."

"Which same their fooling spooked the herd into a stampede," the Kid continued as Dusty paused. "Near on three thousand head went down on to Newton like the devil after a yearling. Seeing them coming riled up the cattle already in the railroad holding pens so that they bust down the fences and the whole damned boiling went through the middle of town."

"Two folks were killed, maybe another dozen hurt, and a helluva lot of damage was done in or around town," Dusty went on grimly. "Paying off for the other stock killed or lost and the damage his herd caused broke the rancher. His crew lost their pay. Two of them got shot trying to rob a store on their way back home. They were broke, damned near starving."

"There's some might say it served them right as they'd been the pair who started the stampede," the Kid drawled. "Only a thing like that doesn't end easy."

"That's for sure," Dusty agreed. "Up to that time Newton'd been a decent sort of town. Folks treated the cowhands fair, everybody got on well enough. Only it stopped after the stampede. Then there was nothing but trouble. They brought in a real mean fighting pimp as marshal, started making fuss with the trail crews. All of it came about just because some stinking yahoo wanted to make a quick profit."

"There's some who'd claim the cowhands didn't have to buy the likker in the first place," Waco said. "Only them who'd say it don't know cowhands and've never driven a trail herd."

"It's not going to happen around here!" Dusty stated, ignoring the youngster's comment.

Except under certain circumstances, Dusty raised no objections to other men drinking. The way he saw it, any man had the right to decide on such matters without interference from others. One of the conditions where he felt liquor had no place was on a trail herd.

Every man of the trail crew needed his wits constantly about him when handling a herd of between two and three thousand head of half-wild longhorn cattle. So drinking and trail-driving did not mix. Most trail bosses banned the carrying of hard liquor—except for the inevitable medicinal whiskey bottle in the chuck wagon—during the drive. Although they frequently complained about the ban, every experienced trail hand secretly admitted its necessity. Cowhands were not saints; their line of work did not call for abstemious, gentle souls. But the majority of them accepted the no-liquor rule when on the trail.

Consequently they built up quite a thirst between towns and, like sailors in port, tended to make up for lost time on their arrival. While not given to drinking in excess, Dusty regarded it tolerantly and as an understandable human failing. What he wished to avoid was the kind of premature drinking which had sparked off the stampede and its consequences in Newton. So far the majority of Mulrooney citizens wanted only to make a reasonable profit from the trail crews and wished to remain on friendly terms with the Texans.

Under such conditions, provided cowhand rowdyism remained in bounds, harmonious relations were assured. From what Freddie claimed, and Dusty had so far seen, the saloons stocked decent whiskey. However cowhands primed on the raw, cheaply-made liquor that Tack's party had brought into town might easily, if inadvertently, spark off an incident that spoiled everything.

"You knew that rancher, Dusty?" Waco asked. "The one in Newton?"

"I knew him. It was Hill Thompson."

" 'Smokey' Hill Thompson, the owlhoot?"

"That's what he became," Dusty admitted. "Like I say, he went broke. The carpetbaggers took over his spread for non-payment of taxes and he went bad. But I knew him in the War, and after. There wasn't a better, stauncher man in a day's long ride."

"You tried to reach him with enough money to pay the taxes, Dusty," the Kid put in. "But he'd shot up that damned State Police posse and gone on the dodge before you got there."

"Thing being, what's to do about that jasper who's peddling whiskey on the ranges out here," Waco remarked, guessing that Dusty wanted the subject closed.

"What'd you suggest we do?" Dusty asked.

"Stop him," the youngster answered bluntly.

"How?" Dusty said.

"How'd you mean, 'how'?" Waco demanded. "Just ride out

there and tell him to quit is how."

"There's no law against selling whiskey," Dusty reminded him.

"Except to Injuns," the Kid went on.

"Yeah," agreed Dusty, eyeing the Kid in a calculating manner. "Except to Indians."

"Now just what've you got in that tricky Rio Hondo mind, Dusty?" the Kid inquired, knowing his small companion pretty well.

"Just a kind of fool notion," Dusty replied. "Let's go see if there's any answer to that telegraph message I sent off this morning, shall we?"

On arrival at the Wells Fargo office they found that an answer had just arrived.

"I was fixing to send it on to you," the agent told Dusty, handing over a buff-coloured official message form.

"Thanks," Dusty answered, then read it.

"Just like back home," drawled the Kid, accepting and studying the paper. "Only I can't see how it helps us."

"It's like you said, Lon," Dusty answered, retrieving the paper and placing it in his vest pocket. "Selling liquor to Indians's plumb illegal. Let's go?"

"Maybe somebody'll tell me what in hell's going on!" Waco yelped as they left the Wells Fargo office.

"I'd surely do it, boy," the Kid replied. "Only I'm damned if I know myself."

3

Prevention Licks Trying to Find a Cure

From behind a rim some three miles outside Mulrooney's city limits, Dusty and Waco watched the Kid preparing to make a purchase. Leaving his huge white stallion well clear of the light two-horse wagon, he walked over and began to talk with the two men. Finding the pedlar who had sold Tack's party the snakehead whiskey had not proved difficult and Waco waited to see what happened next. When sure that the Kid had transacted business with the men, Dusty nodded in satisfaction.

"Let's go, boy," he said.

"I hope this works," the youngster remarked as they walked to where a pair of big, well-made paint stallions stood ground-hitched and waiting.

"And me," Dusty replied. "Prevention licks trying to find a cure any day."

If Abel Hockley had any idea what brought the two lawmen out on a visit to his wagon, he failed to show it. Pocketing the Kid's money, he darted a glance at the burly, buckskin-clad, uncleanly man seated on the wagon box. Then he twirled the stout walking cane in his right hand before resting the tip of its ferrule on the toe of his right boot.

Tall, slender, in his late middle-age, with a lean face that sported a moustache, goatee beard and rat-trap mouth, Hockley dressed in elegant city fashion. Coming closer, Waco studied the man and concluded that the elegance had run to seed. The fancy shirt's cuffs were frayed, the collar dirty, the hat showing much use and boots patched. Thrusting out prominently to catch the eye, the butt of an Adams Navy revolver showed beneath his jacket.

"Howdy," Hockley greeted, watching the two Texans swing from their saddles. "Anything I can do for you?"

"Sure," Dusty replied, letting his paint's reins fall free and walking forward. "Start up that wagon and get the hell away from here."

"How's that?" the pedlar spat out.

"You heard. Take your wagon and go."

"You asking official-like?"

"You could say that."

Hockley's eyes flickered down to the badge on Dusty's vest. Shield-shaped, it bore the words 'CITY MARSHAL, MULROONEY, KANSAS' inscribed on its surface and differed from the star badge used by the sheriff's office. From Dusty, Hockley turned his gaze on Waco. The youngster also wore a shield, but his stated he was a deputy marshal of the same town.

"Don't see any sign of a town hereabouts," the pedlar finally commented.

A town marshal's jurisdiction ended at the city limits. Once past them, he possessed no more authority than any other citizen. Which partly accounted for Hockley's lack of concern at seeing the Texans ride up. Except in the larger cities no licence was required to sell intoxicating liquor. Even if the saloonkeepers in Mulrooney had learned of his activities and objected to losing trade, they had no legal way of stopping him; and if they had, their town marshal could not be used to enforce the ban.

"I reckon you can read," Dusty said, taking the telegraph form from his vest pocket and handing it to the pedlar.

"Sure I can," Hockley growled.

"Then read that out aloud, so's your *amigo* there can hear and understand."

Looking just a touch puzzled, Hockley glanced down at the paper, then stared again and his scowl deepened.

"Marshal Fog, Mulrooney," he read. "Accept your offer. You and all your deputies appointed deputy sheriffs. Letter confirming follows. Bracker, sheriff, Edwards County." Slowly he raised his eyes to Dusty. "So?"

While Hockley understood the message's meaning, he could not see how it affected him. According to what he read, Hockley was facing two men appointed as deputy sheriffs of Edwards County. That meant they could handle law enforcement anywhere within the county's boundaries instead of being confined to Mulrooney's city limits. However he knew his rights and that, unless he broke the law in some way, even members of the county sheriff's office could not order him to move.

Being well aware of the distinctions between county and municipal powers, Dusty had taken steps, on being asked to become Mulrooney's marshal, to ensure he possessed both. That morning he had telegraphed Sheriff Bracker and offered to serve as unpaid deputy sheriff. Clearly Bracker saw the wisdom of such an arrangement and accepted the offer.

"So I'm telling you again to move and keep going," Dusty answered flatly.

If Hockley felt like casting doubts on the message's validity, he restrained himself admirably. To do so would be tantamount to calling Dusty a liar—to which charge a Texan knew only one answer. Instead the pedlar put on an expression of injured innocence and righteous indignation.

"Since when's selling whiskey been again the law?" he demanded.

"Well now, that depends on who you sell it to," Dusty replied.

"How's that?" Hockley growled, tapping the tip of his cane against the boot.

"Like when you sell it to an *Indian* for one thing," Dusty told him.

"I know that," Hockley stated, confident that—for once—he did not contravene the law in such a manner.

Then an uneasy feeling gripped the pedlar; the kind of sensation one got at poker when beginning to realise that what had been taken for a bluff was really a power-packed genuine hand. Noticing the emphasis Dusty placed on the word 'Indian', he turned his attention to his most recent customer.

"My grandpappy's Chief Long Walker of the *Pahnane* Comanche, mister," drawled the Kid.

"And that means you've sold liquor to an Indian," Dusty went on.

"He's no Injun, he's a half-br—!" Hockley began hotly, then clamped his mouth shut so quickly that he almost bit off the end of his tongue.

That tall, dark cuss might look as innocent as a church pew full of choir-boys singing for the bishop, but Hockley was not fooled. Any adverse comments upon his mixed blood would come bouncing back on the speaker's head, followed by something real painful.

"You sold the whiskey to my Injun half," the Kid told him.

Anybody who knew the effect white man's whiskey had upon the red brothers agreed to the wisdom of trying to prevent its sale to them. However the rule hardly applied in the Kid's case. Racial discrimination as such only rarely reared its head on the Western frontier. Cowhands in particular accepted a man for what he was worth, not because of accidents of birth, blood or social standing. If a man of mixed blood lived up to the code of the land, he was regarded as having 'made a hand' and was accepted.

The Ysabel Kid had never been considered as other than a worthy member of rangeland society. That applied even in his border-smuggling days, the running of contraband being regarded in most circles as no more than a protest against an unfair imposition foisted on the public by politicians in far-off Washington. At no time in his hectic young life had he gained a reputation for being dangerous when wet down by fire-water.

Although Hockley did not recognise the Kid, his instincts

27

warned of a trap. Pure coincidence could not have brought the other two Texans along just after he sold the whiskey to the dark youngster. Nor did it seem likely that the two peace officers had guessed, without prior knowledge, at the customer's mixed blood.

Further evidence of complicity flashed to Hockley's mind. In the background, well clear of any lead that might start flying, the peace officers' horses stood range-tied by their hanging reins near to the dark youngster's mount. Yet that huge, magnificent white stallion looked meaner than a bull wapiti bugling for mates in the rutting season. Such a horse would not tamely accept having other stallions so close unless it knew them pretty well.

Which meant Hockley had fallen into a neatly laid trap. If, as he suspected, the saloonkeepers in Mulrooney had sent their law to move him on, he had presented that cold-eyed *big* marshal with an excuse to do so. Should he refuse and be arrested, a jury of Mulrooney citizens could be relied upon to find him guilty. Or so he believed, basing the assumption on how he himself would act in their place.

Anger filled Hockley at the thought of how he had let himself be tricked. The wagon held all the whiskey his bank roll could buy, and which he hoped would realise an enormous profit. On learning of the incident in Brownton which had caused Dusty to leave the town, Hockley had guessed what might happen. Concluding that Mulrooney now stood the best chance of grabbing the trail-herd trade, he established himself in a position where passing customers might easily find him. To be driven off by the law, or arrested for selling liquor to an Indian, would ruin his chances and see him broke. While that would not be an untried sensation, he saw no reason to repeat it. Not when there was an easy way out.

"We can't—talk—about this, now can we, marshal?" he asked.

"How much?" Dusty answered.

"Hell, I don't make much out here—," Hockley began.

"This *hombre* sure lives dangerous," drawled the Kid. "Selling liquor to us poor heathen savages and bribing peace officers."

"I bet he even spits on the sidewalks in Kansas City," Waco went on.

Seeing that bribery stood no chance of succeeding, Hockley decided to make another attempt at straightening out his affairs. In his anger at the possible loss of a good business opportunity,

28

he clean forgot the name he had read on the telegraph form. Or maybe he failed to connect the name 'Fog' with that small, insignificant Texas cowhand.

"Now looky here, young feller—," he said indignantly, raising the walking cane as if intending to make a gesture of pointing it at Dusty. On the wagon box, the burly man tensed slightly.

Springing forward, Dusty lashed out and slapped the cane aside with his left hand. To Waco's amazement, there came the crack of a shot and flame sparked from the bottom of the cane's ferrule. Dusty whipped his right hand upwards, lashing the back of it across Hockley's face. The blow caused the man to stagger and Dusty followed it with a left handed punch to the jaw. Dropping the smoking cane, Hockley sprawled backwards and crashed into the near-side team horse.

At the first movement by Dusty, the man on the box started to rise and draw his gun. Despite being taken by surprise, Waco responded instantly. Down flashed his right hand, fingers closing around the staghorn handle of the off side Army Colt. With the effortless-seeming, but incredibly swift way of a true master, the youngster brought out his Colt, cocked it and fired all in one flowing movement. Before the man's gun could line on any of the Texans, Waco's bullet ripped into his shoulder and knocked him backwards off the box. In falling, he released his hold on the gun. While not as fast as Waco, the man had followed much the same procedure in making the draw, cocking the hammer as the gun cleared leather and squeezed the trigger ready for use. Freed of restraint, the hammer fell before the trigger could return and hold it. So the gun barked and, although the bullet missed, the muzzle-blast's flame burned the off-side horse's rump.

Following his normal type of trading, Hockley often found need for rapid changes of location. So he invariably used a light wagon and selected fast, spirited horses to haul it. Even on what amounted to legitimate trading he and his assistant followed certain precautionary rules. Trail bosses often objected to their men being distracted and sold liquor before the herd was safely penned; and most of them were tough enough to back up their objections. So while Hockley served the customers, the other man remained on the box to control the team while the brake remained open.

At almost the same moment both horses received an unprovoked attack. Hockley's collision with the one at the left caused it to rear, while the sudden burn and sound of the shot set the other plunging forward. Free from impediment by the brake, the wagon lurched into movement and the horses started off across the range at a gallop.

"Stop it, Lon!" Dusty ordered, drawing and lining his left hand Colt as Hockley reached towards the Adams.

"Nigger!" yelled the Kid and his horse started towards him on the run.

One look at Dusty warned Hockley not to continue with his attempt to take revenge. Such speed on the draw only very rarely was achieved without a corresponding ability to shoot accurately and he stood much too close to the other to take chances. So he moved his hand and glanced to where his assistant sprawled unmoving on the ground. Not caring greatly whether the man be alive or dead, Hockley swung his attention to how the Kid was carrying out Dusty's command.

Darting towards the approaching horse, the Kid went into its saddle with a flying bound. Comanche trained, the white would stand indefinitely without being fastened to anything and did not even need its reins left hanging as an inducement to staying put. Clamping his legs about the saddle, the Kid uncoiled the reins from the horn and steered his mount in the direction of the departing wagon.

That enormous stallion could run like a greyhound and found no difficulty in catching up on two harness horses encumbered by even a light wagon. Aware of his mount's potential, the Kid studied the situation and gave thought to obeying Dusty's order. Already the wagon was rolling down a gentle slope, but some distance ahead the ground fell away more steeply. Going down the steep section would be easy enough for a skilled driver in control of his team, yet dangerous when they ran uncontrolled. Anything he aimed to do must be done before they hit that steeper slope.

A signal told the white what its master needed and it lengthened its stride. To the watching men it seemed that the wagon was going at no more than a walking pace, the way the white closed up on it. Drawing alongside the box, the Kid prepared to board it. He took his outer foot from the stirrup, bent his leg under him on the saddle, freed the other boot and hurled himself across the gap separating him from the wagon. Once on the box, he slid the reins from around the brake handle, but made no attempt to operate the lever as an aid to stopping the wagon.

All too well the Kid knew the effect liquor of the kind Hockley sold had upon the drinker. No armchair moralist, he still hated men like the pedlar for what they did to the Indians by selling their poisonous brew. While the man had so far only dealt with cowhands, the Kid did not doubt that he would just as willingly sell his wares to Indians. So the dark youngster aimed to see that the chance did not arise.

Gripping the reins in his left hand, he leaned forward over the box and took hold of the pin coupling the single-tree to the wagon bed. At first he could not draw the pin out and hung in a precarious position as the wagon bounced over the rough ground. Lurching over a rock, the wagon shot forward enough for the pin to come loose and the Kid plucked it out of its hole.

With the team freed, the Kid straightened up again. Flinging the reins and pin from him, he cut loose with a Comanche war whoop loud and wild enough to scare a dead Osage scout white-haired. The yell acted as a spur to send the team horses bound-ing forward at a better pace. Freed from the weight of the wagon, they drew ahead of it although it continued to roll for-ward. Already the incline was growing steeper and the wagon's impetus kept it on the move.

Unguided or not, the team horses possessed sufficient instinct for self-preservation to turn away from the more severe incline ahead of them. Finding no reins-inspired compulsion to continue downwards, they swung off to one side. Without the pull of the horses, the wagon went on its inanimate way guided by the force of gravity.

Coming to his feet, the Kid bounded from the box. He lit down with an almost cat-like agility while the wagon trundled on at an ever-increasing pace. Whistling up the white stallion, the Kid mounted and followed the departing team horses. Be-hind him the wagon careered on downwards accompanied by the jangling clash of breaking glass. Then its near front wheel struck a bigger, firmer rock and shattered under the impact. Tilting crazily, the inoperative remains of the wheel spiked into the ground beyond the rock. Unable to halt so abruptly, the wagon started to somersault over. A hideous cacophony of shattering bottles and splintering timbers rose into the air, making music to the Kid's ears as he caught up to and halted the pair of harness horses.

Curses rose in a wild, almost insane flood from Hockley as he watched the wrecking of his property. However, still covered by Dusty's Colt, he made no more.

"Got the hosses, Dusty," drawled the Kid amiably, coming up to the men. "But dog-my-cats if the wagon didn't sneak away from under me."

"You done it on purpose!" Hockley snarled.

"Did I?" asked the Kid with a mildness of tone that did not match the cold glint in his eyes.

"Damn it, I'll see the sher—!" Hockley began.

"No you won't!" Dusty put in. "Because if you don't pull right out of this neck of the woods, I'll jail you the next time we meet."

"Jail me?"

"That's what I said."

"Do you reckon you can make that selling likker to an Injun charge stick?" the pedlar demanded.

"Maybe I couldn't," Dusty replied. "But you tried to kill me with that fancy cane-gun. That's attempted murder. Fact being no jury'd blame me for killing you defending myself against another try—even if you didn't make one."

"The law—!" Hockley started.

"Doesn't cover what you're doing," Dusty interrupted. "So I'm telling you right now. The next time I catch you selling that snake-head rot-gut to cowhands on the range, I'll kill you where you stand."

Watching the small Texan, Waco could almost believe the threat would be carried out. From all appearances Hockley did not doubt it. All the last attempts at bluster left him. Although the fury and hatred still flickered on his face, it was tempered by fear. However he made a final attempt at putting on a bold face.

"You'll hear more ab—."

It seemed to be Hockley's day to have speeches cut off in mid-sentence. Dropping from his white's saddle, the Kid stepped between Dusty and the pedlar. A face, suddenly changed to a tight-lipped Comanche Dog Soldier's war mask, thrust itself up close to Hockley's and a pair of red hazel eyes glared into his.

"Mister!" said the Kid in a deep-throated *Pehnane* grunt. "You see to your hired man, then climb on to those hosses and get the hell gone from here afore Dusty kills you now."

"Which same I wouldn't want to see him do that," Waco went on. "So I may just have to save him the trouble."

"Which same *I* wouldn't want the boy to have that on his conscience," the Kid stated. "So I just might do it myself."

Looking at the trio of grim faces, Hockley realised that his life had never been in more deadly danger. One wrong move, a further word out of place, could easily bring lead crashing into him. Possibly Dusty Fog would not kill him unless given adequate cause, but the other two might have fewer scruples. With that thought in mind the pedlar started towards the team horses.

"You hired him and got him shot up, mister," Dusty said. "So you see to him now."

Throwing a glance at the groaning, wounded man who was sitting up holding his injured shoulder, Hockley gave a disinterested shrug. "He can go to hell for all of me."

"Take another step and you'll be lying alongside him," Dusty warned as the man continued to walk.

"What the hell do you want now?" Hockley almost screeched, spinning around and glaring at the Texans. "You've come here and busted my wagon—."

"It's called the responsibility of an employer," Dusty answered. "See to that feller. Take him with you—and don't come back."

4

Pick out the Leaders

While Hockley obeyed Dusty and tended to the hired man's wound, Waco went over and picked up the cane. At first glance it seemed ordinary enough, but the weight was more than bamboo, silver decorative connecting bands and a curved walnut handle ought to be. Walking back to Dusty, the youngster turned the cane and looked at the ferrule. A hole of about .36 calibre ran up the centre of the cane, drilled into a steel tube hidden under the coating of bamboo. Closer examination showed rifling grooves cut into the hole.

"That's slick," he remarked, joining Dusty. "I never saw a dingus like this afore."

33

"He counted on it," the small Texan replied and took the cane. "It's a Remington cane-gun. I thought it might be from the way he kept it on the toe of his boot."

"So's he'd not plug the muzzle with dirt," Waco guessed.

"Sure. Although Thomas, the feller who designed this sort of gun for Remington, fitted it with a piece of cork that'd blow out with the bullet and keep dirt out of the barrel. It worked, only it doesn't pay to take chances."

As he talked, Dusty drew back the cane's handle until a flat spring-catch flicked into place and held it open. Then he showed the youngster where to insert the self-consuming paper cartridge and percussion cap. Waco next learned that the tip of the catch holding back the casing could be used as a rear-sight and the location of the small stud which served as a trigger. By the time Hockley had finished bandaging the other man's shoulder, Waco knew how to load and fire the Remington-Thomas Model of 1858 cane-gun.

"Reckon he'll be back, Dusty?" Waco asked as they watched Hockley riding away without attempting to retrieve his hide-out weapon.

"I don't reckon so," Dusty replied and looked at the Kid. "When're you thinking of starting?"

"Huh?" replied the dark young man innocently.

"Work. Earning all the money the tax paying citizens of Mulrooney're going to pay you," Dusty explained.

"Oh, that."

"Sure. I told you to do something, didn't I?"

"I done it. The wagon stopped a mite sudden, but I done it for sure."

"You've done one itty-bitty chore, not a day's work," Dusty told him. "Get on that white goat and go earn your keep."

"Damned if I don't go back to smuggling for a living," grumbled the Kid as he went to his horse. "Leastwise then I'll only do one day's work a day, not three days all rolled into one."

With that he swung into his saddle, saluted Dusty by applying the tip of the thumb to the nose and waggling his fingers. Before the small Texan could make any adequate reply, the white stallion turned and loped across the range. Grinning more cheerfully than he had since learning of the whiskey-pedlar's activities, Dusty walked with Waco to the waiting paints. They mounted and rode back in the direction of Mulrooney.

34

A feeling of well-being and content filled Waco as he rode at Dusty's side through the fringes of the town. Already a good piece of work lay behind them and with the afternoon well advanced he gave thought to the evening. He decided to spend the time improving his relations with Babsy, a pleasant occupation. All such notions departed when, after leaving the horses at the livery barn, he and Dusty arrived at the marshal's office. They found Big Sarah standing at the desk, feeding shells into one of the ten-gauge shotguns from the wall rack. Relief showed on the woman's face at the sight of the Texans.

"I'm sure pleased to see you, Cap'n Fog," she stated.

"What's up?" Dusty asked.

"Shamus O'Sullivan, Fritz Voigt and Frenchy Rastignac're down at the Fair Lady with their gang of gandy-dancers, fixing to hang a railroad lamp outside the front door."

Such an action might not appear a cause for alarm to some people, but Dusty knew it to be a situation calling for immediate action. Hanging the lamp outside the saloon signified that the railroad workers considered it to be their private domain. Any cowhand who saw it would regard it as a challenge, an infringement on their liberty, and feel compelled to take up the matter.

"Let's go talk to them about it," Dusty said. "Put up the scatter, Sarah."

"I don't reckon I'll be needing it now," grinned the women, removing the shells and returning the gun to the rack.

On the way along the street Dusty explained the seriousness of the situation to Waco.

"How'd we handle it?" the youngster asked.

"That depends on how they want to play it," Dusty replied. "The first thing to do when you're handling a crowd gathered for fuss is to pick out the leaders and deal with them. This time we know their names. You won't always have that much of a start. So we'll play it like we don't and see how you get along—if there's time to do it, that is."

While Dusty realised the gravity of the affair, he did not forget that his only backing was a youngster inexperienced in the work of a peace officer. He knew Waco to be brave and not likely to panic, but wanted the youngster trained as a lawman. So he was prepared to delay dealing with the gandy-dancers, railroad construction workers, long enough to give Waco a practical lesson.

"Maybe I should've loaded up that fancy cane-gun and

35

brought it along," Waco said with a grin, having left the weapon at the office.

"That'd be as much use as an udder on a bull," Dusty replied. "If you figure on quieting a crowd, tote along a ten-gauge scatter-gun. One look at those big black-eyed barrels and it's surprising how peaceable folks can get."

Arriving in front of the Fair Lady, Dusty and Waco paused to look through the window. There being only the gandy-dancers present, Dusty delayed his entrance while Waco gained experience.

Some twenty men of European extraction had gathered before the long mahogany bar. Ignoring the very attractive sight of Freddie clad in her working clothes, or Babsy dressed saloongirl fashion, Waco studied the men. Three caught his eye, being in the centre of the crowd and in conversation with Freddie.

Holding a railroad engine's lamp was a big, brawny black-haired man so obviously Irish that he might have been painted bright shamrock green. To his left stood a blond, crop-headed German almost as large. At the right of the trio, the third of Waco's selection looked almost weedy compared with the other two, being shortish, slender man of Gallic appearance. Yet something about him made Waco regard the third man as a leader rather than one of the led.

"Good choosing," Dusty complimented when Waco pointed out the trio. "I'd say you called them right."

"As right as the off side of a hoss," agreed Sarah. "Those three used to come in while the town was being built and what they said went with the rest of the rust-eaters."

"Then they're the ones we'll dicker with," Dusty said. "Leave me do the talking and start the doing, boy."

"Sure," Waco replied, too impressed by the serious way the other spoke to make any further comment.

Followed by his two deputies, Dusty stepped through the bat-wing doors. What he heard on entering showed him that they had come not a moment too soon.

"I tell you, Miss Freddie," O'Sullivan was saying, waving the lamp. "With this here hanging out front all the cowhands, buffler-hunters and other riff-raff will know this's under railroad pertection."

"And I'll lose their trade," Freddie replied.

"Divil the bit," O'Sullivan assured her. "We'll let it be knowed

36

that any as wants can come on in—As long as they treats you civil and don't get under our dainty lil feet."

"Hey, Shamus," Voigt hissed in a dramatic stage-whisper, nodding towards the batwing doors. "Just take a look at what's come in."

"Sure, and 'tis a cowhand," the burly Irishman said, after directing a long stare at Dusty. "But what's that thing on his vest?"

"A badge, *mon ami*," Rastignac told him.

"So it is. Now there's an evil thing somebody's gone and done, pinning a great, big, heavy badge on him that ways," O'Sullivan commented. "And what can I be doing for you, me lad?"

"I hear tell you're fixing to hang that lamp outside," Dusty replied.

"That we are."

"You know doing it'll mean trouble?"

"Not as long as what it's there for's respected by one and all," O'Sullivan answered.

"You know it won't be," Dusty pointed out. "And that being the case, I'm not letting you hang it."

"*You're* not?" Voigt growled.

"You caught on real fast," Dusty drawled.

"Just how do you and your deputy there aim to be after stopping us then?" demanded O'Sullivan, nodding in Waco's direction as the youngster stood behind Dusty with hands thumb-hooked into his gunbelt.

"Any way we have to," Dusty assured him. "Stay here as long as you like. Have your fun, but don't try hanging up that lamp."

"And if we says we're going to hang it, regardless?" asked O'Sullivan, then answered the question. "I suppose you'll put lead into us?"

"You reckon you could stop us without them guns?" Voigt inquired.

What happened next handed the gandy-dancers the surprise of their lives. Reaching down, Dusty untied the pigging thongs holding the bottom of his holsters to his legs. Just as unconcernedly he unbuckled and removed the belt, handing it to Freddie. Then he looked at the trio and grinned.

"They do say showing licks telling about it, and proves more," he said.

"You means to rassle with us?" O'Sullivan gurgled in a disbelieving tone.

"I'd prefer it one at a time," Dusty replied. "But that's your choice."

"One at a—!" the Irishman croaked, eyes bugging out while his companions stared in speechless amazement at the small Texan.

"It'll have to come sooner or later," Dusty told them. "So we might just as well get it over with right now."

"And no hard feelings at the end of it, win, lose or draw?" O'Sullivan wanted to know.

"Like you'd say, devil the bit of it," Dusty answered. "If you win, the lamp goes up. If you lose, it doesn't."

"And fairer you couldn't be," boomed the Irishman. "We'll let Pierre here give you the first whirl."

"That's the only fair way," Voigt agreed.

"As long as he doesn't hurt me," finished Rastignac with a wink, peeling off his jacket.

Taking in the Frenchman's slight build, it seemed strange that he should be one of the leading lights of a hard-muscled, brawny gang of gandy-dancers. Any thoughts that Dusty might have had on Rastignac being merely in such an exalted position by virtue of friendship with O'Sullivan and Voigt ended at his selection to fight first.

Quickly a circle formed, large enough to permit the fighters plenty of moving space. Waco stood by Freddie's side and exchanged a glance with her, both wondering if Dusty might be biting off more than he could chew. For his part, Dusty concentrated on studying his opponent and noting certain significant details.

From all appearances, Rastignac knew more than a little about fist-fighting. He adopted the ready stance rapidly replacing the old bare-knuckle style in pugilistic circles back East, right fist cocked ready, left held across to guard his jaw. However he appeared to have learned the style badly, for his foot placement might have been faulted by a purist. Although positioned about a shoulder's width apart, the left foot at the rear pointed sideways instead of both being aimed to the front.

If Dusty noticed the apparent fault, he overlooked it. In fact he showed very little sign of being ready to defend himself. Grinning confidently, Rastignac prepared to attack. Only he did not use his fists. Up lashed his left foot, rising with speed, power and skilled precision. Always before his *savate* attack had come as a complete surprise when used against men unaware of the French Creole style of foot-and-fist fighting.

Unfortunately Dusty not only knew of *savate*—including how its foot placement differed from ordinary boxing—but possessed a real good method of countering the attack. On a visit to New Orleans in the early days of the Texas Republic, Dusty's uncle, Ole Devil Hardin, had met and hired a small Oriental man most folks thought to be Chinese. Actually Tommy Okasi hailed from the Japanese Islands and brought with him certain strange skills. To Dusty alone of the Hardin, Fog and Blaze boys, Tommy had passed on the secrets of *ju-jitsu* and *karate*, alien fighting arts virtually unknown at that time in the Western Hemisphere.

Faced by such an attack many men would have tried to grab the leg, but Dusty knew a far better—and safer—way of dealing with it. Swiftly he brought his hands down, crossing his arms just above the wrists. Instead of making an attempt to catch the leg, he allowed it to pass into the lower section of the X his arms formed. Only when the kick's upward rise had been blocked and brought to a halt did he make the next move. Catching hold of the toe of Rastignac's boot in the right hand and its heel in the left, Dusty gave it a surging, twisting heave. A howl of mingled pain and surprise broke from the Frenchman as his other foot left the floor. Unable to stop himself, he somersaulted over and landed with a thud that drove all wind or cohesive thought from his body.

"I'd say it was you next, mister," Dusty remarked, looking at Voigt.

The soft-spoken words cut through the excited chatter of the crowd and silenced it. While the gandy-dancers had expected Dusty to tangle with Rastignac, although not with the result just witnessed, they had doubted if he would take on either Voigt or O'Sullivan.

"Don't you b'ar-hug him too hard, Fritz," warned one of the crowd. "You'll likely squeeze him in two halves."

"I just give him *ein kleine bischen,* make his eyes pop out of his head and break a couple of ribs," Voigt answered. "I'm not wanting hurt a lawman too bad."

With that the German advanced on Dusty. It seemed that the small Texan did not take the threat too seriously, for he moved to meet Voigt. Watching them, Freddie sucked in a deep breath and opened her mouth to give a warning. Having seen Voigt

39

give a man *ein kleine bischen* bear-hug, she knew just what it meant. Yet Dusty made no attempt to avoid the reaching arms. In fact he appeared to walk straight into them. Although unused to opponents willingly entering his grasp, Voigt did not intend to look a gift-horse in the mouth. Curling his brawny arms around Dusty's torso, he prepared to give a crushing pressure.

"Oh lord!" Freddie breathed, wondering what had prompted Dusty to act in such an apparently reckless manner.

She learned quickly enough.

Like his every action since entering the room, allowing Voigt to gain the hold fitted into Dusty's plan. He knew that for the most part the gandy-dancers were not gun-fighters and displaying superlative skill in that respect would have only a subsidiary interest for them. Proving that he could beat them at their own style of fighting was the way to deal with them. Once that had been established, he figured there would be no trouble keeping the railroad workers' high spirits within bounds.

Although Dusty allowed Voigt to obtain the bear-hug, he made sure that his own arms stayed outside the other's grasp. That did not worry Voigt—at first—for he reckoned the agony of his pressure would prevent his victim doing anything effective. Which theory might have worked better had it been given a chance to mature. Even as the brawny arms started to tighten about his middle, Dusty cupped his hands and clapped them over Voigt's ears.

In making the move Dusty tried to achieve a compromise between too little power and striking so hard that he burst the German's ear drums. It seemed that he succeeded. On the hands slapping home, Voigt's body went rigid and his arms relaxed. Thrusting the German away, Dusty followed up with a style of attack none of the watchers had ever seen. Although he drove his hand into Voigt's belly, he did not close it into a fist. Instead he used the *hira nukite*, the level-piercing hand of *karate*, taught to him by Tommy Okasi. With the fingers extended and together, thumb bent across the palm of his hand, Dusty stabbed Voigt full in the solar plexus. An explosive croak broke from the German and he staggered back, holding his middle as he folded over. Again Dusty struck, still with his hands held in that alien manner. Only this time he chopped the heel of each palm into the sides of Voigt's neck, tumbling the man to the floor like a back-broke rabbit.

40

"Now there's something you don't often see," Freddie commented, first of the audience to recover from the shock of seeing Voigt's dreaded bear-hug broken with such ease.

"He's a tricky one for sure," O'Sullivan agreed, a shade uneasily.

"Two down and one to go," Dusty drawled.

Realising what that meant, O'Sullivan gave rapid thought to his social position. He held an enviable standing among the gandy-dancers, being known as their unofficial leader. Many concessions came his way from the bosses of the construction crews, in return for which he maintained a form of law and order among the other workers. Such a position came and was retained by his ability to beat his companions physically. Should he tangle with the small Texan and be bested, the loss of prestige would have a serious effect on his standing. Yet refusing to take up the challenge was just the same.

Although not a man given to deep thinking, O'Sullivan could on occasion make a rapid decision.

"Sure and we all know you can fight, friend," he said, waving a hand to his fallen companions. "So let's try something different, shall we?"

"Such as?" Dusty inquired.

"A friendly game of 'Douse-The-Candle'."

A faint grin twisted Dusty's face at the Irishman's suggestion, for he knew it meant a rougher version of wrist-wrestling. While Dusty's knowledge of *ju-jitsu* and *karate* gave him an advantage in a straight fight, he knew that he stood no chance at all in the contest O'Sullivan suggested. So did the majority of the crowd and one member of it in particular.

Standing unnoticed on the stairs, ready to help if the need arose, Mark Counter decided the time had come for him to intervene. Not that he would have gone unnoticed without such a centre of attraction as Dusty's actions offered. Six foot three in height, golden blond curly hair topping an almost classically handsome face, Mark stood out in any crowd. Great shoulders, hinting at the enormous muscular development underneath, spread wide the material of a costly, made-to-measure shirt. From there he tapered down to a slim waist and curved out to long, powerful legs. Along with his green silk bandana, all his clothing hinted at wealth. The gunbelt about his middle, carrying ivory-handled Army Colts in carefully tooled holsters, told

41

another story. Although showing the finest 'Best Citizen's Finish' Colonel Colt's Hartford factory could produce, the revolvers were purely functional fighting weapons, hanging just right for rapid use.

Dandy dresser the elegant blond giant might be, but he possessed few peers in the various cow-land arts. Third son of a big South Texas ranch owner, rich in his own right since a maiden aunt died and left him her considerable fortune, Mark still preferred to ride as a member of Ole Devil's floating outfit. Nor did his sartorial tastes make him a less useful member of that efficient fighting force. Few who saw him in action during a rough-house brawl soon forgot the scene. Already his great strength had become legendary. Calamity Jane often told how he single-handedly lifted her wagon out of a gopher hole* and performed other feats of muscular prowess in her presence†. Nor did Miss Martha Jane Canary for once stretch the truth. Riding as he did in the shadow of the Rio Hondo gun wizard, Mark's ability with his Colts rarely gained its just acclaim. Yet many gentlemen experienced in such matters put him second only to Dusty Fog in speed and accuracy. Anybody who took Mark Counter for no more than a dandy stood a good chance of regretting it.

However Mark did not appear to be in a position to make his full contribution to the affair at that moment. He had been shot in the shoulder during a brawl on his arrival in Mulrooney. While Waco's intervention had prevented any further injury, the blond giant's left arm hung in a sling. For all that he moved forward.

"Don't you reckon Dusty's just a mite light to take you on at 'Douse-The-Candle'?" he asked, elbowing through the crowd

"And who asked you to bill in?" O'Sullivan demanded indignantly, swinging around to see who was interfering.

"I'm Dusty's deputy," Mark replied. "So I reckon I can take some of the work off him."

"With a busted wing?" O'Sullivan asked, nodding to the sling.

"I only use one hand for 'Douse-The-Candle'," Mark told him. "If you don't mind, it'll be my good one. Get the candles out and lit, then let's give her a whirl."

*Told in TROUBLED RANGE.

†Mark's other meetings with Calamity Jane are told in THE WILDCATS, THE FORTUNE HUNTERS, THE BIG HUNT and GUNS IN THE NIGHT.

"Mark!" Freddie gasped. "You may burst open your wound."

"Nope," he grinned. "I'm fixing to use my other hand."

Once again O'Sullivan assessed the situation. While a defeat over the small Texan might save his face, he knew there would be sceptics who commented on the disparity between their weights. Although slightly smaller than Mark, he weighed a little heavier and did not figure there ought to be too much trouble in licking the blond Texan.

"I'll douse it quick for you," O'Sullivan promised and nodded to Freddie. "Could we trouble you for two candles, ma'am?"

Taking seats on opposite sides of a small table, Mark and O'Sullivan waited for the final preparations to be made. Collecting two candles from the bar, a gandy-dancer lit them and dribbled wax on to the table to hold them in position where the contestants' hands would arrive at the conclusion of the bout. Then Mark and O'Sullivan placed their right elbows on the table and interlaced fingers.

"Start us off, Miss Freddie," Mark suggested. "If that suits the Irish gent here."

"It'd be a honour," O'Sullivan answered. "Go to it ma'am."

"I'll count to three and say 'go,'" Freddie told them. "One—two—three—go."

Instantly O'Sullivan started to press at Mark's hand, with the intention of forcing it down on to the flickering candle flame. Already the Irishman had felt the hard solidity of the Texan's hand, but did not expect any great difficulty in forcing it over. Only that did not happen. Instead he met a rock-like resistance that refused to yield.

Around the table startled exclamations rose from the gandy-dancers. Sitting up, groaning and holding his head, Voigt muttered curses in German. However Rastignac caught him by the arm, helped him rise and pointed to the table. Any ideas the German might have formed about resuming hostilities with Dusty ended. Sinking into a chair, he accepted the drink Babsy brought and watched the game of 'Douse-The-Candle' run its course.

Slowly the confidence oozed from O'Sullivan's face, being replaced by a mixture of strain and amazement. No matter how much pressure he exerted, he could achieve nothing. Then slowly but inexorably Mark started to force the Irishman's hand down. Not that he brought an end to the game immediately. Twice

O'Sullivan strained every muscle to bring his hand to the vertical. Then slowly it sank a few inches. Gathering in his reserves of strength, Mark threw it all into a final effort. Down went O'Sullivan's hand, crushing the reduced candle under it and dousing the flame.

"The saints preserve us!" the Irishman yelped, shaking his hand in an attempt to restore life into it. "If you can do that with one arm in a sling, bucko, I'd hate to see what you can do when well."

"I've never met a man who came so near to licking me," Mark replied. "This calls for a drink, I'd say."

"That it does, that it does," O'Sullivan agreed. "And I reckon seeing's how you've bested us, we'll not be hanging the lamp—."

"They've not bested us all!" put in the youngest member of the railroad men, and the only one to wear a gun in a holster tied to his leg. "We come here to hang that lamp and I'm going to do it."

"The hell you are, Wicker!" O'Sullivan growled.

"Don't you or anybody else try to stop me!" Wicker warned, hand hovering with spread fingers above his Colt's butt. "I'm taking that lamp and hanging it just like we planned."

At which point Waco became aware that Dusty had not yet strapped on his gunbelt. For once the small Texan had failed to take the elementary precaution, feeling there would be no need for guns with the situation so well in hand. He also knew that it was too late to rectify the mistake. Then Waco took the matter out of his hands.

"Come ahead," the young Texan said. "All you have to do is pass me."

5

You'll Never Know How Lucky

With that inborn instinct all westerners gained, the crowd knew what it must do. So gandy-dancers and saloongirls fell back, standing well clear of the two young men. Much as Dusty wanted to interfere, he knew he could not without implying a lack of trust in Waco. At the small Texan's side, Freddie watched with a growing feeling of concern. Not that she feared for Waco, having seen how fast he could draw a gun. Inexperienced she might be, but she guessed killing the gandy-dancer would make trouble. Maybe not that night, but later it would be remembered and Wicker, despite being the aggressor, raised to the status of a martyr. Freddie could still remember the expression on Waco's face as he burst into the saloon to kill the man who shot Mark. Unless she was very mistaken, only the blond giant's intervention had prevented more of his attackers from feeling the youngster's lead. So when Waco gave out his quiet challenge, she expected the worst.

"You reckon I can't pass you?" Wicker snarled.

"That's for you to find out," Waco answered.

Much of Wicker's time had been spent in practising his draw and he expended hard-earned money on fodder for his Colt. Like most youngsters of the day, he revelled in stories of the great gun-fighting names and longed to emulate their achievements. Working among gandy-dancers offered few chances to display his talents, for they tended to be fist- or knife-fighters, with various erotic variations thrown in. At last he found himself faced with the real thing, in the kind of position he had dreamed about.

Only a nagging doubt bit into him. Apart from a very few cases, western peace officers received their appointments by virtue of exceptional gun-skill. So far two of those Texan John Laws had proved more than able to handle the best the railroad could offer. Maybe the tall, blond youngster came up to their high standard in his own line. However Wicker did not wish to back down.

"I'm coming!" he warned and hoped his voice did not sound as strained to the others as it came to his ears.

"Come or go," Waco answered evenly, raising his right hand to wave at the lamp. "But that dingus stays right whe—."

Sensing the chance Waco's action offered, without having the knowledge or experience to question it, Wicker stabbed his hand down at his gun. While such a move might pass as fast when performed against his even less skilled gandy-dancer admirers, it failed to come even close to the standard required when used against Waco.

45

At the other youngster's first movement, Waco sent his left hand from hanging with deceptive negligence at his side to around the near Colt's butt. Out came the gun and roared while Wicker still tried to draw his clear of its holster.

There had been a time, not too long past, when Waco would have killed Wicker on the spot. Only since meeting Dusty Fog he gained a slightly higher opinion of the value of human life. When he stepped in between Wicker and the lamp, Waco did so out of a sense of duty. He knew neither Dusty nor Mark could stop the young railroad worker at that moment and so moved in to do so. And he came prepared to halt Wicker any way he found necessary. Instinct and knowledge told him of Wicker's indecision, allowing him to gauge the other's true potential.

So, instead of planting the .44 bullet in Wicker's body, Waco drove it into the boards between his feet.

Shock numbed Wicker at the sound of the shot and he stared with unbelieving eyes to the smoking Colt in Waco's left hand. Even as he watched, the Colt performed a pinwheel on the young Texan's forefinger and flipped back into its holster all in one continuous move.

"Still fixing to come on?" Waco asked.

"And that he's not!" O'Sullivan put in grimly. "Give it up, Wicker lad. We've had our fun and nobody's been hurt—."

"Speak for yourself, *mon ami*," Rastignac put in, rubbing his rump and wincing. "I'll never be the same again."

"There's some'd say any change'd be an improvement," O'Sullivan sniffed, then went on. "None of us's been hurt bad. Let's keep it that way."

"Mick's right," Freddie continued. "Donna, pour out a round of drinks on the house. Then for Pete's sake let's start making some money."

The prospect of free drinks prevented any comments on Wicker's failure as a gun-fighter. Gathering at the bar, the gandy-dancers reached for the glasses which Donna's deft hands filled. O'Sullivan turned and grinned broadly at Dusty.

"You'll be taking something with us, marshal?"

Before Dusty could answer, cowhand yells and drumming hooves sounded on the street outside. Giving a shrug, the small Texan nodded towards the doors.

"Some other time, Mick. Right now I've got to go earn my pay. Let's go see who it is, Waco."

46

"There goes a real big man, and I'll lick the pants off anybody who says different," O'Sullivan boomed, then nodded to Mark. "Well, almost anybody."

"You'll get no argument on that from me," the blond giant answered, watching his companions leave.

"And you leave off that damned gunbelt, Wicker boy!" O'Sullivan growled, turning to the young railroad man who stood clutching a whiskey glass in a hand that shook a trifle. "You're lucky not to've been shot."

Thinking of how Waco had been when they first met, Mark nodded in sober agreement.

"You'll never know how lucky," he said. "Set up another round on me, Donna!"

"And when you've done it, you're going back to bed," Freddie whispered into his ear.

"The night's young—," Mark began.

"I could always have the girls undress you and carry you there," Freddie smiled. "And you know they'd do it if I told them."

Recalling how the girls had pitched into the bunch of buffalo-hunters who tried to cause trouble on the day he arrived, Mark did not doubt that.

"Maybe I should stick around," he suggested. "That Wicker kid might get all liquored up and try something loco like looking for evens. I don't reckon Waco'd hold back twice."

"I didn't think he'd hold back once," Freddie confessed. "Don't worry about Wicker. I'll make sure that he behaves."

"Reckon you can?"

"Do *you* reckon I can't?" countered Freddie. "Go on, that fool trick you pulled took more out of you than you're wanting to show."

Which, being the truth, Mark conceded. Guessing he could safely leave matters in Freddie's hands, and hearing nothing to tell him he might be needed in the street, he returned to his room upstairs and went to bed. Although Wicker drank enough to raise his courage, he did not commit such a foolish act as going after Waco to resume hostilities. At the first hint that he might, Freddie gave Donna a signal and herself carried the drink the bar-maid—as Freddie called the female bartenders—had prepared to the young man. Flattered by the attention, Wicker drank it. Shortly after he fell asleep and did not wake until back at the

47

construction camp. There, giving the matter sober reflection, he decided that he lacked the necessary ability to make a gun-fighter and stopped trying.

While Waco heard nothing of it, he probably saved a young life on his first day as a deputy. If Wicker had continued trying to pass off as a proddy gun-hand, he would have eventually met a man with less scruples than the young Texan and gone the way of the foolhardy.

Any hopes Waco nourished of asking for Dusty's opinion of his conduct in the saloon died as they reached the sidewalk. Down before their office almost all of Colonel Goodnight's JA trail crew milled horses in the centre of the street. Forcing his mount from among the others, one of the cowhands drew his revolver and rode towards the office.

"Let's get the town clowns out here and show them that the JA's arrived, boys!" he whooped.

Before either Dusty or Waco, running along the street, could intervene, a screech, like a cougar finding the wild hogs had ate its young might give, rang out. Hurling from the shadows at the end of the jail, the young cowhand Tack bounded on to the hitching rail and from there flung himself at the potential window-breaker. As he hooked one arm around the offender's neck, Tack used the other hand to knock up the revolver and its bullet sped harmlessly into the air. Then the two of them slid from the bucking horse, landing on the ground as it went off along the street.

"Best catch it, boy," Dusty said. "I'll go talk some to them."

An enraged cowhand sat up, cocking a fist ready to strike at his attacker. Then recognition came and he held off the assault long enough to demand an explanation.

"What in hell fool game you playing at, Tack?"

"I'll tell what!" the window's defender yelled back no less heatedly. "I done dug a hole with a shovel to earn enough to pay for that glass and stuck it in with my own two lily-white lil hands. So I'll be tarnally damned if I'll see it all busted up again."

"How come you-all took to digging and fixing windows, Tack boy?" asked a grizzled veteran of the cattle industry. "Don't Colonel Charlie pay you good enough without that?"

"The marshal here allowed that I bust it and he didn't like sitting in a draughty office," Tack replied.

"You mean that there marshal got all mean 'n' ornery?" demanded another of the cowhands. "Made you ride the blister end of a shovel and fix up a window that got busted accidental-like."

"He for sure did," grinned Tack, seeing Dusty approaching.

"Such doings should be stopped instanter-like!" stated the cowhand Tack had pulled from his horse.

"Or even sooner," continued yet a forth hand. "Where-at's this mean ole Kansas lawman?"

"Coming up right now," Tack informed him, delighted with the way things were going.

Although the trail crew turned with some hostility to face the approaching lawman, much of it died away on seeing him. While the sun had gone down, the street was sufficiently illuminated for them to tell that no ordinary Kansas trail-end town marshal was coming their way. Nor did Dusty's small size fool cold sober cowhands, even those who did not know him. All knew they faced a master of their trade and a man more than ordinarily competent in handling his guns. Any faint doubts which may have lingered fled as the oldest cowhand present spoke.

"Air that you, Cap'n Fog?"

"This's me," Dusty agreed. "And I'm town marshal here."

Even those of the trail crew who did not ride with Goodnight on the third drive to Fort Sumner had heard of Dusty Fog. The men who made the drive recalled him all too well and knew better than cross his path in what he considered to be his duty.

"That danged Injun never allowed that you was marshal," the old timer said aggrievedly. "And me sharing my makings with him."

While the Kid delivered news of Brownton's peculiar ideas, he had failed to mention who ran the marshal's office in Mulrooney. Questioned later on the lapse by the indignant old timer, he replied, "I figured you'd learn soon enough."

Rising and dusting his clothes, the potential window-breaker studied the front of the office and exclaimed, "I never see a finer piece of glass-fixing. It'd be plumb sinful to destroy a work of art like that."

"Which same I'm scared of riling Cap'n Fog as well," grinned the old timer. "So I per-poses, seconds and thirds that this-here fool meeting adjourns to the hotel, sees Colonel Charlie for our

49

pay and goes out to spend it. If we're going to wind up in pokey, let's get good and drunk first."

"Go to it," Dusty told them. "Only keep your guns in leather and horses on the streets."

With that he stood aside and watched Waco hand over the runaway horse to its owner. Exchanging laughter and cheerful comments, the trail hands followed the old timer on his way to carry out his suggestions.

"It's going to be a lively night tonight, boy," Dusty told Waco as they watched the departure. "And afore it's through you'll wish you'd six arms and at least eight legs."

"Did I do right, facing down that young cuss at the Fair Lady?" Waco asked a touch worriedly.

"Do you reckon you did?"

"I figured that he had to be stopped."

"You figured it right and acted righter," Dusty assured him. "Sure he had to be stopped. But if you'd thrown that bullet into him, the gandy-dancers'd've remembered it. They'll not forget the way you acted either, and it'll pay better than shooting that fool kid. Now they know how well you can handle a gun—and that you know just how much to use it."

"What now?" asked the youngster, looking relieved at receiving Dusty's approbation. He had been worried about how the small Texan might regard his actions in dealing with Wicker and felt satisfied now he knew.

"We'll grab a meal and do like I said in the Fair Lady, make a start at earning our pay," Dusty replied.

"Now me," Waco said. "I'd reckon we've already done pretty fair at that."

With the meal over, Waco began to find out just how much work a conscientious peace officer did in a day. A marshal of Wild Bill Hickok's type spent most of his time sitting in card games, or loafing in a favourite saloon, only appearing if called upon to quell a disturbance. Wyatt Earp became conspicuous only when little danger threatened, he had plenty of tough backing, and somebody of importance was on hand to witness his 'heroics'. Although not a professional lawman, Dusty had been trained to try to prevent trouble breaking out, rather than arrive and attempt to halt it once started.

So he and Waco took to the streets, keeping an unobtrusive but unceasing watch. The youngster, cowhand at heart, bewailed the fact that nobody had warned him that being a deputy entailed so much foot-work or he would never have taken the fool chore. He also listened as Dusty explained the various specialised aspects of what they did, whether it be breaking up a fight or something which, on the face of it, appeared to be the most simple routine.

"Try that door," Dusty told him as they walked by a warehouse near the railroad depot. "Make sure it's locked."

"Sure," Waco replied and started to obey.

"Hold it right there!" Dusty snapped as the youngster reached towards the door's handle.

"What's up?" Waco hissed, right hand fanning gun-wards.

"Suppose there's somebody inside, robbing the place," Dusty said, walking forward. "He hears you trying the door and figures its a watchman, or somebody coming and throws lead. What'd it do to you, stood where you are?"

"Make a hole in my fool hide, I reckon," Waco answered as he studied his position in relation to the door. "Only there's nobody inside."

"If there is, time you've learned different it's too late. No matter whether you're certain the place's empty, always stand to the side and reach around to try the door. That way you stand a better than fair chance of being missed if anybody is inside and cuts loose.'

"You must reckon I'm awful green."

"Sure. But I figure you've got good enough sense to learn."

"What happens if somebody's inside and shoots?" Waco asked after moving to the wall and reaching around to try the door handle.

"A whole lot depends on how many of 'em you reckon're inside and if you've got an amigo with you," Dusty replied. "If the place's only one room and the door's weak enough, bust in fast with a gun in your hand."

Continuing on their way, Dusty explained other matters arising from Waco's question. Always eager to learn, Waco listened and stored the knowledge away for future use. In later years, as an Arizona Ranger, county sheriff and finally U.S. marshal,* he found Dusty's teachings invaluable and following the precautionary rules laid down by the small Texan often saved his life.

*Told in SAGEBRUSH SLEUTH, ARIZONA RANGER, WACO RIDES IN THE DRIFTER and HOUND DOG MAN.

Not wishing to crowd too much detail on to the youngster at one time, Dusty failed to mention one elementary, but vital, rule. Knowing Waco's ability in the line that rule covered, he felt that no explanation would be needed. Later events proved him wrong.

6

Innocent as Lon Looks,
or Guilty-Looking as Hell

"I tell you, Lon, this here's a fool, no-account, no-good chore," Waco stated as he walked with the Ysabel Kid through the rear streets of Mulrooney on the morning of his second day as a deputy marshal. "Damned if being a lawman's not worse than following a plough or herding sheep."

"Now me, I wouldn't know about that, not having done either of 'em," the Kid replied.

"No, and you didn't do none of the walking last night!" yelped the youngster indignantly. "All you done yesterday was bust up some poor feller's wagon and trail 'round the country bumming smokes offen cowhands. Ole Dusty made me *walk* near on a hundred miles. We stopped cowhands shooting up main street, gandy-dancers and buffalo hunters chawing each others' ears off in fights, toted drunks to jail. Then what happens?"

"You tell me," suggested the Kid, having returned at midnight from spreading the word about Brownton's welcome to various trail drives.

"I'll tell you for sure!" Waco yelled. "That mean boss we got hauls me out of bed near on at day-break, when I figured that being a peace officer I could sleep town hours, and has me help get all those jaspers we'd stowed away in the pokey on their feet."

"They'd got to clean out the cells afore going afore the judge. Or would you want to be the boy who does it?"

"Like ole Pickle-barrel says, they mussed 'em up, leave them do the cleaning," Waco answered, referring to the swamper from the Fair Lady Saloon who had been hired by Dusty to act as jailer.

"Then what's gnawing at your craw, boy?" grinned the Kid, knowing just how little the youngster's complaints meant.

"So we has them get everything good and clean. Comes time for them to go to court and I'm figuring on riding a chair at the back while the judge fines 'em— So then what does Dusty say?"

"I'd never guess."

"He says, 'You and Lon go take a walk around town!' That's what he says. 'Take a *walk*,' he says. And me with a damned great slab of crowbait just eating up hay and corn like it's going out of fashion, then getting all feisty through not being rid. Dammit, I walked all around this town last night."

"It looks better in daylight," commented the Kid.

"Nothing looks better when you're walking!" Waco objected.

Despite his complaints and protests, the youngster knew why Dusty had given the order. The time might come when their lives would depend on knowing what lay behind the buildings of the main street, or how to reach a particular part of town by an inconspicuous route. Which gave a serious purpose to the stroll without lessening his objections to performing that most distasteful business, walking.

So far only a portion of the buildings were occupied, the original settlers having combined their resources to erect properties for sale to people attracted by their town's prosperity. Dusty had sent out his two deputies to learn which places were still empty and note the location of tempting prospects for robbery.

"There's one place we shouldn't need to worry about," the Kid remarked, nodding to a good-sized house standing in a large square of land surrounded by a picket fence.

"That's for sure," Waco agreed. "They're starting to fix it up."

"They never waste any time," the Kid replied.

Several women wearing nuns' clothing worked around the property, digging the ground or tidying up the outside of the building. Waco strolled over to where a small novice was applying white paint to the picket fence.

"Howdy, ma'am," he greeted. "You-all settling down all right?"

Although the girl turned a pert face towards him, she did not offer to reply. A shadow fell across the fence and Waco found that another member of the convent had come over. The newcomer equalled big Sarah in size and heft, had a face with strength of will and humour in its lines and wore a slightly different style of habit to the novice.

"We're under a vow of silence here, young man," the big woman told him in a broad Irish brogue. "So Sister Teresa's not allowed to answer you."

"Thanks for telling me, ma'am."

"But how come the vow doesn't apply to me?" smiled the woman. "That's what you're wondering, isn't it?

"Yes'm," admitted Waco with a grin.

"Somebody has to deal with people from the outside, and it falls on the senior sister until the mother superior arrives. You're one of the town marshal's deputies, are you?"

"Sure, ma'am."

"Tell your marshal that if he needs any help I can give to come and ask."

"I'll do that, ma'am," Waco promised and rejoined the Kid. "What do you reckon to that, Lon. These gals aren't allowed to talk."

"I've heard tell of it afore, down in Mexican convents," the Kid replied. "Come on, they're one bunch who won't concern us."

After touring the convent's side of the town, Waco and the Kid swung over to the other section beyond the railroad tracks. There they saw what they regarded as an ideal site for a brothel; not knowing that Freddie, realising the need would arise for such an establishment, had planned the placing of the building with that use in mind when helping to lay out the town.

Before going back to the office, the deputies called in at the livery barn to check on their horses. Another large corral next to the barn's sizeable compound held the stock of the town's freight company. Halting to look over the harness horses, they leaned against the corral fence.

An old timer carrying a dinner-pail in one hand and coffeepot in the other came through the alley between the barn and the freight outfit's warehouse. Ambling up to the deputies, he directed a spurt of tobacco juice into the water of the horse-trough halfway between the corral and the building.

"Danged uppy shiny-butts," he said.

"Who, us?" asked the Kid.

"Naw! Them two milk-faced dudes up to the office there. Can't leave all their fool paper-work to go out and eat, so I have to tote it to them. Which same I wouldn't mind if the office was on the ground, but I have to go up them steps to hand it over."

Following the direction of the oldster's indignant glare, the Kid and Waco looked to where a flight of stairs led to a first floor outer door.

"Sure is a sinful sin, brother," the Kid declared.

"You never said a righter word," the old man agreed and walked slowly away. Then he halted and looked back. "That safe they've got up there's mighty strong. You boys don't need to stand guard on it."

"That went right by me," the Kid replied.

"Didn't you know? They've got a big old Chubb safe up there to hold the company's wealth."

"We didn't know," admitted Waco.

"I wouldn't've mentioned it, only you pair being lawmen it's all right."

"Let's hope nobody else mentions it," the Kid said as the old man continued his interrupted delivery. "I reckon Dusty'll want us to keep an eye on the back here, safe or no safe."

On hearing about the safe, Dusty confirmed the Kid's guess by telling them to make periodic checks on the rear of the freight outfit. Not that they needed to start right off, first they could relax at the office and clean the weapons—Winchester rifles, shotguns and a long-ranged Sharps buffalo gun—supplied for their use.

The rest of the day went by without serious incident. Hearing from the first arrivals of the fair manner in which the town was run, other trail crews held down their boisterous behaviour to reasonable levels. As for the railroad workers, the story of how the law had handled O'Sullivan's gandy-gang lost nothing in the telling. No other construction crew felt like chancing such leniency should they cut up extra rough.

During the day three separate visits were made by citizens of Brownton, all with the intention of studying the situation. Their findings caused some alarm and despondency, also a desire by a number of citizens to migrate to Mulrooney's richer pastures.

At noon on the third day Waco accompanied Dusty and the other deputies to meet the east-bound train on its arrival from

Brownton. There the youngster saw how Dusty dissuaded various unwanted elements from taking up even temporary residence after their desertion of what they regarded as the other town's sinking ship. After some very plain talk from Freddie Woods, who came along to give civic approval of Dusty's actions, a madam called Lily Gouch received permission to buy the property selected as a brothel. Other business people also gained access, but a number of petty crooks, card-sharks and confidence tricksters continued with the train when it pulled out. During the weeding-out process, Waco saw Dusty apply an iron fist without a velvet glove and learned from the sight.

One man who arrived from Brownton not only received admittance but, despite being a professional gambler, was made welcome. Having known Frank Derringer as an honest player and friend, Dusty offered to take him on as a deputy marshal. Among Mulrooney's civic ordnances, one gave the marshal's office the right to examine any gambling device and to order its destruction should it prove dishonest. While a straight man himself, Derringer knew how to detect crooked moves or equipment as a means of self-defence. His agreement to Dusty's suggestion not only put a valuable weapon in the hands of the law, but paved the way for Waco to gain a very thorough knowledge of all aspects of gambling.

Although he had an arrangement to take Babsy on a buggy ride that evening, the first opportunity to present itself since becoming a deputy, Waco agreed to accompany Dusty and Derringer to an inspection of the gambling devices at the Fair Lady and Wooden Spoon—the only other saloon yet open. The tall, slim gambler fixed his badge to the lapel of his black cutaway jacket. He wore a white broadcloth shirt, string tie, striped trousers and town boots, while an ivory-handled Army Colt hung in a tied-down holster on his right leg. Unless Waco missed his guess, the gun had seen some use.

"Where's Lon?" Derringer asked as they left the office.

"Down to the store teaching the owner how to shoot," Waco replied.

"Lon giving shooting lessons?"

"Why sure. He allowed it to be his civic duty to help a tax-paying citizen learn how to defend hisself—and that Sarah Birnbaum's a right pretty lil gal."

Which explained the Kid's eagerness to instruct Storekeeper

Birnbaum in the art of handling a gun.

A trio of men rode by Dusty's party and swung their leg-weary mounts in the direction of the Wooden Spoon Saloon. Although Waco studied them as they passed, he attached little importance to their arrival. Unshaven, clad in range clothes that showed hard wear and each with a low-hanging gun at his side, to Waco they looked just like the majority of trail hands who came north with the herds. Nor did he read any significance in the way they tossed their reins over the hitching rail on dismounting, instead of fastening them to it. Most of Clay Allison's crew did the same, in case a very hurried departure should be necessary.

However the youngster noticed one thing of interest. In the days when he rode for Clay Allison, the sight of another man's horse about to throw a shoe would not have passed without comment. As a deputy marshal he felt that he ought to warn the man in case the deficiency had not been detected.

"Hey, mister," he called, moving slightly ahead of his companions. "Hold it a min—."

At the first word the three men turned. They had already left the horses and were about to step on to the sidewalk. Surprise flashed on to the faces of the two outside men at discovering that the two cowhands and professional gambler they had passed wore law badges and were coming towards them. Although at first the centre man showed no concern, his companions clearly had no desire to make the acquaintance of peace officers. Both immediately started reaching for their guns and he followed their lead.

Two things kept Waco alive that day; Dusty's knowledge of a lawman's most basic rule and the small Texan's ambidextrous prowess.

"Look out, boy!" he yelled, thrusting Waco aside with his right hand while the left flickered across to the butt of the off-side Colt.

For all that Waco came close to death.

Although last of the trio to start moving, the centre man beat the other two to the shot. Flame ripped from the barrel of his Colt and the bullet missed the staggering youngster by inches. If Dusty had failed to recognise the danger, or had moved less rapidly, the lead would have torn into Waco's body. Before the man could change his aim or fire again, Dusty's Colt barked and he shot to kill. There was no other way. Already the man had shown considerable ability at throwing lead and proved he had reason to fear the approach of law enforcement officers. Taking chances with such a man paid off only in grieving kin-folks and tombstones. So Dusty sent a .44 calibre conical bullet into the man's head and ended his menace instantly.

While the centre man might be good, his companions came nowhere near his standard. Counting himself no better than fair, Derringer still outclassed them and he stood third on the law's side.

Off balance and staggering, Waco partially repaid his error by beating Derringer and the remaining two men into action. Bringing out his right hand Colt, he cut loose and nailed the man at the left through the shoulder. As his victim spun around, Waco did no more than thumb-cock the Colt and ignored the fact that the other still held a gun.

Then the youngster learned his second lesson in a few seconds, although it had been one Dusty had failed to mention on the first evening outside the warehouse. Swinging his Colt, Dusty sent a shot into the wounded man as he hung against the hitchingrail and tried to lift his gun. Dusty acted fast, without a moment's concern for the other's condition and was fully prepared to continue shooting if the situation warranted it. However the impact of the second bullet made him open his fingers and the revolver fell to the ground. For a moment the man hung on the rail, then slid downwards. Startled by the shots, the three horses bolted.

An instant after Waco fired, Derringer brought up his own Colt. Having time to spare, even though it amounted to no more than a split second, he angled his shot to injure rather than kill. Letting out a screech as lead burned into his shoulder, the third man jerked backwards. His feet struck the sidewalk and he sat down on it. Hurt or not, he showed a remarkably quick grasp of the situation and threw his gun aside. Nor did he act a moment too soon, for Derringer knew the rule of a peace officer which Waco had yet to learn.

"Don't shoot!" the man yelled, clutching at his right shoulder with the left hand. "Don't shoot. I'm done."

"Move in on them and watch them good," Dusty ordered and, as they advanced, went on, "Boy, never as long as you're wearing a lawman's badge call out to a man you don't know, or go towards him after you've stopped him, without being ready to draw your guns."

"I only—," Waco began.

"I know what you aimed to do and don't blame you for doing it. But innocent as Lon looks, or guilty-looking as hell, don't make the mistake of not being ready to draw. And if you have to throw down on a man, keep shooting at him as long as he holds his gun no matter whether he's standing or lying."

Cold-blooded it might seem, but the advice proved valuable to Waco in later years. The youngster had killed four men already, but each time in a plain shoot-out and never when working as a peace officer. So, despite Dusty's assumption, he did not know the rule every successful western lawman followed.

A crowd quickly gathered, bursting out of the Wooden Spoon or dashing along the street. Leaping from the sidewalk, some cowhands caught the fleeing horses and led them back towards the saloon. Ignoring the questions fired his way, Dusty told Waco and Derringer to gather up the trio's weapons. While that elementary precaution was being taken, he studied the trio. The first man lay dead, a hole between his eyes mute testimony to Dusty's deadly skill. Although hit twice, the second time in the chest, the next man might pull through if given medical attention soon enough. Due to Derringer's consideration, the third member of the party had no more than a minor wound. Though he would not be able to handle a gun for a spell, he would live. Something more than the wound seemed to be bothering the third man and he looked at Dusty.

"How'd you know?" he whined and released his shoulder to point at the dead man. "Stayley there reckoned word couldn't've got here."

While not sure what the man meant, Dusty decided it might be worthwhile trying a bluff to learn.

"It arrived."

"Th—The money's in Stayley's saddle pouches. All of it. Just like when we took it out of the Wells Fargo box."

"Where was that?" Dusty asked.

"Six miles south of Newt—," the man began, then chopped off his words as he realised that Dusty ought to know the answer.

"A Wells Fargo coach, huh?" Dusty said thoughtfully.

"I've got nothing to say," the man replied.

Guessing that he would learn no more at that moment, Dusty

let the matter lapse. If it came to a point, he did not want the matter aired in public.

One did not need to be a genius to guess what had happened. After robbing a Wells Fargo stagecoach close to the town of Newton, the trio had come to Mulrooney. From the condition of their horses, they had made a fast ride. Probably their intention had been to mingle with the other visitors until after the hunt for them died down. If they had kept their heads when Waco called to them, the plan would have stood a better than fair chance of working. No word of any hold-up had reached Mulrooney and, despite noticing the way in which they had left their horses, Dusty had no cause to suspect them of breaking the law.

7

Maybe you Didn't ask Him Right

Coming up at a run, the Ysabel Kid saw there would be no need for his intervention. Before he could return to continue sampling Sarah Birnbaum's cooking, he found himself actively involved. Dusty told him to see to the removal of the body, guard the doctor while the two wounded men received attention and to make sure that the trio's horses went into the civic pound for disposal.

"Would that be all, Cap'n Fog, sir?" he asked, seeing chances of further culinary pleasures disappear.

"It'll do for starters," Dusty replied. "Waco, fetch their saddlepouches with you while we go over the Wooden Spoon's games. Then we'll see what that jasper was talking about."

While Dusty felt certain there would be no cause for complaint, he insisted that the examination of the saloon's gambling equipment be carried out. Later, when other places opened, he wanted proof that he had dealt in the same manner with everybody. He wanted to learn more about the stage hold-up, but could not make a start until after the men's wounds had been treated. So he might just as well fill in the time usefully. However, to prevent accusations at a later date, he took the precaution of fastening and sealing the saddle pouches in the presence of the saloon's owner—a member of the town council—and did not trouble to look into them before doing so.

After the check, which proved negative but gave Waco a chance of learning something of crooked gambling, Dusty left the saloon ready to investigate the activities of the trio before they came to Mulrooney. However Mark brought news that sent them to look in on a private card game at the hotel. The game proved dishonest and the ensuing formalities further delayed Dusty's plans. In addition the Kid had not yet returned from the doctor's office with either of the wounded men. So Dusty locked the saddle pouches in the safe and sent the old jailer to telegraph the authorities at Newton, requesting information about the hold-up.

Although it was Waco's night off watch, and ignoring the fact that he had a date to take Babsy for a buggyride, he remained at the office to watch Derringer demonstrate the operation of various crooked gambling devices found at the hotel. So engrossed did the youngster become that he arrived late at the rendezvous, sparking off a quarrel with the pert little blonde that later proved to have most beneficial results.

It seemed that the fates conspired to prevent Dusty satisfying his curiosity. The doctor, new from the East, young and very keen to aid suffering humanity, put both wounded men under such heavy opiates that even the lighter injured of the pair would not be able to speak before morning. Realising that the doctor had acted as he thought for the best, Dusty withheld the blistering comments which rose at the news. All he could do was telegraph Sheriff Bracker at the county seat and ask for information on a man called Stayley.

As things turned out, the doctor's actions did not delay the investigation. A Texas rancher noted for his rivalry with Colonel Goodnight arrived with his herd and paid off his trail drive crew. Only unceasing vigilance by Dusty and all the available deputies prevented trouble breaking out between the two groups of celebrating cowhands. So there would have been no chance of interviewing the men, even if either could have talked.

Next morning, leaving Derringer and the tall, lean, leather-tough old jailer known as Pickle-Barrel to deal with the ordinary overnight prisoners, Dusty prepared to interrogate the man wounded by the gambler-deputy. Brought from the doctor's house while still unconscious, the man had been held in one of the three single-bunk cells reserved for dangerous prisoners. When the Kid fetched him into the office and seated him before Dusty's desk, he looked pale but in reasonably good condition apart from his wounded shoulder.

Studying the lean face, with its hooked nose, rat-trap mouth and weak chin, Dusty could not place it with any outlaw of his acquaintance. Not that he felt too surprised at the failure. While he possessed a fair knowledge of Texas law-breakers, he had not previously found the need to familiarise himself with the Kansas crop. Nor did the office possess anything that might help make the identification. In a well-established town, a new marshal might expect to find a collection of wanted posters gathered by his predecessors. Mulrooney had not been built long enough to accumulate such aids.

"How's the shoulder?" Dusty asked.

"It hurts like hell. Are you turning me loose?"

"Nope."

"Why're you holding me?"

"Don't you know?" asked Mark, standing at the man's right side while the Kid hovered at his left.

"What's your name?" demanded Dusty before the man could reply, sitting on the edge of the desk in front of him.

"Tom Smith."

"I met one of your kinfolks," drawled the Kid. "Only you don't feature him."

"Not enough to be real close kin," agreed Dusty. "Would Smith just be your summer name?"

"Summer and winter both," the man replied, gaining confidence as he took in the youthful appearance of the trio. "What'd you fellers start shooting at us for yesterday?"

"To stop you throwing down on *us*," Dusty replied. "Why'd you do it?"

"Maybe he figured you'd recognised him from his picture on a wanted dodger, Dusty," Mark suggested.

"You ain't seed no picture of me on a dodger," Smith stated, with such confidence that the Texans believed him.

"Not even for that stage hold-up six miles south of Newton?" Dusty asked.

"How'd you mean, marshal? I don't know about no hold-up any place."

"Did Stayley?"

"I only met him on the trail into town. When you three fellers jumped us, I figured you must be some fellers looking for evens with him."

"Then why'd you draw?" Mark said.

"Wouldn't you? Hell, those three fellers'd seen me ride in with Stayley. They'd not wait to ask who I was afore shooting."

Clearly the delay had given Smith a chance to think up excuses for his actions. Dusty had feared that it might, but had hoped the opiates would keep the man unconscious long enough to prevent him examining his position. However Dusty felt that he ought to be able to learn enough by careful manipulation of the man.

"Let's take a look at those saddle-pouches, Mark," the small Texan ordered. "Lon, go ask Dongelon to come over and check the seals before we break them."

After the owner of the Wooden Spoon arrived and made sure that the seals placed on in his presence still remained intact, Dusty opened the first of the pouches. A low curse broke from Smith and he started to rise as Dusty tipped the contents on to the desk. Nor did the man alone show surprise, for nothing more important than a heap of newspapers slid into view. Only for a moment did the shock crease Smith's face, then a calculating glint replaced it and he sank back into the chair.

"Where is it?" Dusty demanded, after the other pouches and the trio's bed-rolls had failed to yield anything incriminating.

"Where's what?" Smith countered innocently.

"You expected the money to be in there," Dusty said.

"Me? I didn't expect a thing."

"Then why did you tell us that Stayley had it in his saddle pouch?"

"I must've been out of my head with pain. Getting shot makes me that way."

"Do you get shot often?" Mark wanted to know.

"Naw! Why should I?"

"Now me," drawled the Kid. "I allus shoot owlhoots."

"I ain't no owlhoot!" Smith yelled and a foxy grin creased his face. "Say, if there was money in Stayley's pouches, maybe you bunch took it."

"Now you don't mean that like it sounds, do you?" asked the Kid, his bowie knife sliding from leather.

"I was only joking," gulped Smith, turning his eyes from a face that no longer looked young to an eleven-and-a-half inch long, two-and-a-half inch deep, razor-edged blade.

"Don't joke with us!" Dusty barked. "We don't joke with thieves."

"Could be he's innocent, Dusty," Mark suggested.

"I've been telling you that I am!" Smith wailed.

"I believe you, like I believe in Santa Klaus and fairies," stated the Kid.

"You'll let me go then?"

"Well no, I can't say that I will," Dusty replied. "See, you nearly shot a deputy out there. So I'm holding you for attempted murder."

"I never got off a shot!" Smith squealed.

"Can you prove it?" drawled the small Texan.

Smith gulped down something that appeared to be blocking his throat as he realised that he could not. Only his companions, neither of whom could testify, and the peace officers knew exactly what happened outside the Wooden Spoon. If the marshal and his deputies claimed that Smith had fired at the young one, a jury of town folk would believe it.

"If you aim to railroad me, I'm in no shape to stop you," Smith said.

"I'm right pleased you know it," Dusty replied. "Put him back in his cell."

Watching the man led away, Dusty felt puzzled. The discovery that the pouches held no money had come as a surprise to Smith. Yet, after one brief show of emotion, he had settled down and seemed almost content with his position.

"What do you make of that, Dusty?" Mark inquired, returning from locking Smith in the cell.

"Something stinks about it. He almost looked happy when he saw the money'd gone. Why in hell doesn't Wells Fargo in Newton answer our telegraph message?"

If the men in question had heard Dusty's words, they could not have answered any more promptly. The office door opened and a youngster entered carrying an envelope.

"This message just come in, Cap'n," he said. "The agent told me to get it over here as fast as I could."

Taking the message form, Dusty learned why Newton had delayed in answering his request for information. A stagecoach carrying ten thousand dollars had left Newton heading south. Attempts to contact the way station at which it would halt for the night had failed due to the telegraph wire being down. Alarmed by the message Dusty sent, a posse rode out along the stage trail. They found the telegraph wires had been cut and, re-establishing contact with the way station, learned the coach had not arrived. By that time a careful search could not be made, but men went along the trail. Pure luck led them to where the coach had been driven into a dry wash, its dead driver and guard being inside and the horses taken away. Finally the Newton agent requested that Dusty held Smith until their special investigators could come to Mulrooney and interrogate him.

"And that's just what we'll do," Dusty told Mark.

At which Waco made a belated appearance and told the others that one of the vacant saloons was being taken over by its new owner.

"We'd best go look them over," Dusty said. "Hey, Pickles!"

"Yo!" replied the jailer entering the office.

"Be real careful with that jasper in the solo cell. He's likely mixed up in a stage robbery and double killing."

"I'll watch him with both eyes," Pickle-Barrel promised.

Although he had been employed in the menial task of swamper at the Fair Lady, the old timer had proved to Dusty's satisfaction that he possessed the required attributes for a jailer. Actually Pickle-Barrel had only taken work as swamper until his present position became available. He had scouted for the Army until rheumatism slowed him down to a point where further work of that nature would be suicidal. However he could still take care of himself in a tight corner and knew all the safety precautions to take when dealing with dangerous prisoners.

After introducing himself to the newly arrived saloonkeeper, a big, buxom woman called Buffalo Kate Gilgore—whom he had last seen operating a place in Brownton—Dusty watched her meeting with Freddie Woods and sensed rivalry in the air. However, he guessed Kate could be relied upon to keep a straight place and did not foresee the extra work the rivalry between the two women would give him.

A meeting with the various trail bosses and town's leading citizens followed, to arrange for means of entertaining the cowhands on Sunday without opening the saloons. Between them Dusty and Freddie had already formed a plan. While the term 'rodeo' was not yet in use, they used many of the contests such affairs would later offer as a means of letting the cowhands show various skills and find work to occupy otherwise idle and mischievous hands.

On his return to the office, Dusty found a big, bluff-looking man waiting. Dressed in a town suit and boots, although the tie had been removed and a Stetson hung on the peg by the door, the newcomer gave the impression of spending much time out of doors. A Remington Army revolver rode a crossdraw holster at his left hip and a county sheriff's badge glinted from his vest.

"Cap'n Fog?" the man asked, a faint hint of surprise in his voice. "I'm Tom Bracker."

"Howdy, sheriff," Dusty replied, shaking hands. "Hope I haven't kept you waiting for too long."

"Pickles's been showing me over the place. It's a right good lay-out. Whoever planned it knew what they was at."

"That was Mayor Woods."

"It figures. That's one smart lady—and a real looker too."

"They don't come prettier, or smarter," Dusty agreed.

"How's the town settling in?" Bracker inquired, taking the seat Dusty offered him.

"Fair enough. Not many places open yet, but Kate Gilgore came down from Brownton. Likely there'll be more."

"Knew Kate back in Hays. She runs a straight place. That's more than you can say for the rest of the Brownton bunch. Say, I looked in on that Smith jasper. Can't say as I can place him."

"Does the name Stayley mean anything to you?" Dusty asked.

"Don't it to you?" Bracker inquired.

"Nope."

"If it's who I reckon, Joe Stayley, you've picked up a three thousand dollars bounty—and a peck of trouble."

"Is he wanted that bad?"

"He is up here and out to Montana. He's Tricky Dick Cansole's right bower."

"Tricky Dick?" Dusty repeated. "I'm sorry, sheriff—."

"Make it 'Tom'."

"Running trail herds in didn't give me any call to know your Kansas owlhoots, Tom."

"I thought Tricky Dick was better known than that," Bracker mused. "Likely it's only a matter of time afore he is. He's real smart, works with a small, hand-picked bunch and's pulled off some nifties."

"That Smith *hombre* doesn't strike me as top-grade stock," Dusty commented.

"Or me," the sheriff admitted. "You say they came straight over here from a hold-up. Did they have any money along?"

"The saddle-pouches where it was supposed to be came up empty when we opened them."

Apparently the news did not surprise Bracker, for he merely nodded. "That's Tricky Dick's way all right. Every time his bunch pull a robbery, the fellers who do it stash away the loot someplace safe and ride hard. Then if they get caught, they've nothing to prove they did it. Thing I don't get is why Stayley grabbed for his gun when your deputy shouted to him—Sure, Pickles and Frank Derringer told me how it happened."

Thinking back to the incident, Dusty found various facts leaping to mind. "The other two made the opening moves," he said. "Once they'd started, what else could Stayley do but back them?"

"Not much," admitted the sheriff. "Only why did the others make the play?"

"I've got a feeling that at least Smith didn't know the money'd gone. If he didn't, he wouldn't want a lawman searching them as the money'd give them away."

"You mean that Tricky Dick aimed to double-cross them?"

"If nothing worse."

"It could be," Bracker said thoughtfully. "Or he hadn't used them before and didn't want them knowing too much about how he worked until he knew them a whole heap better."

"I don't know enough about this Tricky Dick to start guessing which one's right," Dusty said. "Say, you'll have time to identify Stayley if we go now. They haven't buried him yet."

"Let's go take a look," Bracker offered. "I've only seen his face on wanted dodgers, but I've got one with a good description of him along."

Going to the undertaker's parlour, the sheriff and Dusty arrived only just in time to view the last remains before the coffin lid was screwed into place. To give him his due, the undertaker had done a good job and the lawman studied the ashy-pallid face.

"It's Stayley," Bracker stated, comparing the features with the wanted poster he held. "Whoever made this drawing's good.

That's three thousand dollars your office's picked up."

"We made an arrangement with Freddie Woods," Dusty answered. "All bounties go into the civic funds."

Bracker nodded approvingly. "I've never been much on taking them myself. Say, about that money. Have you talked to Smith about it?"

"Nope. Trouble being by the time we got around to it, he'd thought up some slick excuses for what happened.'

"How come?"

"One thing and another kept coming up. You know how it is in a trail-end town like this. Half or more of the time you're wishing you'd a regiment of deputies on hand. Like I said, by the time we got around to him, He'd thought up the answers."

"Maybe you didn't ask him right," growled the sheriff.

"With a feller from the *Kansas City Intelligencer* in town?" Dusty asked mildly. "That'd be buying trouble."

A point which Sheriff Bracker understood all too well. Being a 'liberal' newspaper, the *Intelligencer* looked after the underdog's interests. A favourite target for the paper was any peace officer who rough-handled criminals; though the liberal-intellectuals who ran it never gave space to the brutal treatment honest Texas cowhands received from the Earps or others of their kind. Backed by a number of influential men at the state capital, possibly so that they would not become targets for its attacks, the *Intelligencer* could easily blast the career of any peace officer it crossed. Dusty's prominence on the Southern side during the Civil War, along with the fact that most of his deputies hailed from Texas, made him a likely target for *Intelligencer* investigation. In which case Bracker did not wish to become involved in the process of asking Smith 'right'.

Although no liberal-intellectual, Dusty did not approve of the beatings or torture many peace officers of the day used to extract information from captured outlaws. Not that he regarded criminals as misunderstood victims of circumstances who needed only understanding and kindness to turn them into useful citizens. While that might be true in a few cases, most men took to crime in their ways. However he realised that rough-handling a prisoner made the victim look sympathetic to the public and only rarely produced any useful results.

Having seen Belle Boyd, the legendary Rebel Spy, interrogate a prisoner and having discussed the subject with her,* Dusty knew of far more subtle ways than the crude methods most peace officers employed to gain information.

"We'd best leave him to the Wells Fargo fellers," Bracker remarked as they walked back to the office. "Anyways, I don't reckon he's important."

"He could be real important to Tricky Dick," Dusty replied.

"How come?"

"It's just a hunch, but I think Smith's counting on his boss to get him out of jail."

"Why?" Bracker demanded.

"Because Smith figures he's the only one with any idea where the money from the hold-up might be. That's why he's sitting quiet instead of telling us all he can to get even with Tricky Dick for double-crossing him."

Before Dusty could go further into his idea, a man dashed up to say a fight had broken out in the Wooden Spoon. So the two lawmen headed in that direction and temporarily forgot the possibility that Smith was guessing correctly.

8

Nobody's Taking my Guns

"Damn and blast all women!" Waco growled bitterly, slipping a combustible cartridge into the chamber of the Remington cane-gun taken from the whiskey pedlar. "If it wasn't for them, I could be out watching the fun instead of sitting my butt-end down here, cleaning guns."

"Women're the cause of all the trouble in the world," Dusty told him, entering the office.

After breaking up the fight at the Wooden Spoon, Dusty and Sheriff Bracker grabbed a meal and prepared for more work. If the previous nights had been rowdy, Saturday out-did them all. Every member of the marshal's office staff and Bracker found

*Dusty's meetings with Belle Boyd are in: THE REBEL SPY and THE COLT & THE SABRE.

69

plenty to do. Any ideas the sheriff might have brought with him about needing to teach the Texans practical law enforcement ended rapidly. In fact he soon saw that he was working with masters of his trade. Another thing to strike him was the air of friendly enjoyment shown by visitors and residents alike. Due to the early spadework put in by Dusty and the deputies, Mulrooney already bore a reputation as a fair, tolerant place, yet capable of halting anybody or outfit that went too far.

Finding none of the veiled hostility and open money-grabbing of other trail-end towns, the cowhands reciprocated by keeping their fun within bounds. Hard workers, they played just as energetically. If a rope, horse or gun formed a frequent aid to their fun, it was because in many cases the cowhand owned nothing else. With money in their pockets, gained by gruelling hours of hardship on the way north, they sought only to enjoy themselves. The more they had to pay for damage caused, the better time they felt they had had. If, as often happened, the cowhand went broke, he could ride south and find food offered in exchange for information by the trail crews on their way to the rail head.

Dusty knew all that and explained it to the Mulrooney citizens. In their turn, they showed tolerance and accepted a few broken windows or disturbed sleep as the price for making a good living out of the trail herds.

Of course there were incidents which wound up by one or more of the revellers being hauled off to jail, but Bracker saw no objections raised to that even by the arrested parties' friends.

Although Mark had volunteered to keep the office on Sunday, while the rest of the Texans, Big Sarah and Pickle-Barrel went out to keep the peace among the folks attending the various sporting events, things did not work out as planned for Waco. A pretty, vivacious little red-head from Buffalo Kate's saloon became attracted to the young deputy, which almost sparked off a hand-scalping brawl with Babsy. In the interests of peace Dusty sent Waco back to the office and kept the two girls well clear of each other.

Figuring that the Wells Fargo special agents would come in on the afternoon train, Dusty left the sporting events in good time to meet them at the office. He found Waco in a dark humour, somewhat disgruntled with women in general and Babsy in particular. While waiting for his companions to return, the youngster had passed his time by cleaning the office's assault armament.

While the cane-gun did not come into that category, it stood on the rack with the rifles and shotguns. Dusty intended to take it south with him as a present for his uncle. The time might come when Ole Devil, confined to a wheel-chair since failing to ride the paint Dusty now used as a personal mount,* might find a need for such a device. So, after completing the others, Waco attended to it.

"Did anything else happen down there?" the youngster asked, fitting a percussion cap on to the nipple.

"I managed to keep them apart, if that's what you mean," Dusty grinned. "Damned if you're not worse than ole Mark, way you get the gals fussing over you."

"All I wanted was a peaceable afternoon," Waco objected, reversing the cane and fixing the open screw-in ferrule to the mouth of the barrel.

"Which's what you've had," Dusty pointed out, sitting behind the desk.

Footsteps sounded on the sidewalk and two men walked by the office window, then halted at the door. Waco laid the cane on the desk top and perched his rump on the edge, then looked as the door opened. While the men who entered wore town suits and derby hats, they had weather-beaten faces and sported range-fashion gun-belts with Army Colts in tied-down holsters. Nor did Dusty find the contrast incongruous. A Wells Fargo special investigator might work out of one of the big city offices, but he spent a good proportion of his life in the open and exposed to the elements.

"Howdy, marshal," greeted the taller man, advancing to the desk. "I'm Haver and this's Tarrick. We're from Wells Fargo."

"I've been expecting you," Dusty answered, rising to shake hands. Then he sat down again, expecting the men to ask for information.

"We've come for that feller you took prisoner," Tarrick told him. "So if you'll turn him over to us, we'll tend to his needs."

"Suppose you gents show me something to identify yourselves first?" Dusty countered.

Anticipating the request, Haver had already reached into his jacket and produced a wallet. He slid it across the desk and it fell to the floor on Dusty's side. Even as Dusty bent over to pick it up, certain facts sprang to mind. He recalled how the two men

*Told in THE FASTEST GUN IN TEXAS.

had darted glances around them on entering, almost as if they feared a trap might be laid for them. More significant, for men in their position learned the value of remaining alert, neither had made any mention of the money. It almost seemed that Tarrick knew such a question would be a waste of time.

Even as the thought struck home and Dusty started to straighten, he found it came too late. Haver's right arm bent, elbow pressing against his side. Instantly a Remington Double Derringer shot into his palm, propelled there by a device like the spring card hold-out machines used by crooked gamblers. Strapped around the wrist and hidden by shirt or jacket sleeve, the hold-out machine usually carried selected cards or a pre-arranged deck to be brought into play at a favourable stage of the game. It also could be made to hold a small hide-out gun, a fact Dusty knew but had overlooked until too late.

"Come up slow and easy, marshal," Haver ordered. "And you sit still, or he gets it, young feller."

While Waco might have only recently learned one important rule concerning firearms, he needed no telling when to sit tight. Bucking the odds at that moment would have been fatal, if not for himself, to Dusty. So he remained seated on the edge of the desk and kept his hands motionless. Any hope of making a move lessened as Tarrick's revolver slid from leather and lined on the youngster.

"What now?" Dusty asked, obeying the order by coming erect at a leisurely pace.

"Like Tarrick said, we'll take your prisoner—," Haver replied.

"Which of you's Tricky Dick?"

"Neither of us, short-stuff," grinned Tarrick. "And we ain't Wells Fargo men, comes to that."

"I'd figure so much for myself," Dusty admitted.

"No sir. We left 'em with bust heads in the men's room at a whistle stop down the tr—."

"Shut it, Walt!" growled Haver. "And you pair shed your guns."

"Nobody's taking my guns," Dusty answered quietly.

"We are," Tarrick told him. "Off your body if you make us."

"Go right to it," Dusty replied, using the same even tone. Only you hit me any place other than between my two eyes and I'll take at least one of you with me before I go."

"The shots'll bring folks running," Waco went on.

"That's one thing we don't need to worry on," Haver answered. "Near on everybody's out back of town. The railroad depot crew could hardly wait to see the train off and get out there."

"Time anybody gets back, you'll both be wolf-bait," Tarrick put in.

"You're still not taking my guns," Dusty warned.

For all the calm manner in which he spoke, Dusty did not make the mistake of underestimating the danger. Seated behind the desk with his knees in the roomy leg-hole, he could not hope to draw his guns quickly enough to save himself. Yet he had no intention of surrendering them to the two men. Doing so would in no way alter their plans if they meant to kill him.

The matter went deeper than that. While law enforcement in the West might tend to be disorganised, already a tradition had grown among the better class of peace officers that a lawman must never surrender his gun. Trained in that belief, Dusty intended to force the issue and hope for a break. Not that getting one was likely when dealing with such men. A Remington Double Derringer lacked accuracy, but across the width of the desk could plant its fat .41 calibre bullet into a man-sized target easily enough.

"Hell, Dusty!" Waco put in. "There's no sense in getting killed to hold that Smith jasper. I say hand him over."

"The kid's showing sense, marshal," Haver commented. "Let the gunbelt drop, boy, then go and do it."

"Sure," the youngster answered, still sitting on the desk but unbuckling his belt. He nodded to the cane-gun and went on, "I near on got my leg bust in a fight at the Fair Lady last night and can't stand on it too good. I'm riding that walking-cane to get around. Which's why I'm here 'stead of out watching the fun."

"Don't try anything smart like sliding that belt to your pard," Haver warned, darting a glance at the cane and seeing nothing suspicious.

"Not me!' Waco promised and lowered the belt to the floor at the side of the desk.

"Happen you've got any ideas about whomping me on my pumpkin head with that cane, forget 'em," Tarrick continued.

"Mister," the youngster replied, lowering himself carefully from the desk like a man with an injured leg and casually gripping the cane, "that's the last thing I plan to do."

With that he lifted the cane from the desk, lining it by instinct like hip-shooting a Colt, and pressed the stud trigger.

At first Dusty had been taken in by Waco's acting, so well did the youngster play the part. Not until the mention of the fictitious injury did the small Texan guess what his companion had in mind. Studying the two men, Dusty saw no hint that they failed to accept Waco's behaviour as genuine.

Maybe Haver or Tarrick would have been more suspicious if Waco was older, a professional gambler instead of an obvious cowhand, or the normal type of trail-end town lawman. The Remington-Thomas cane-gun helped with the deception by virtue of its design and special features. Although its tip pointed towards the men and could be easily seen, no hint of its deadly nature showed. Most such items on the market bore a wooden tampion to act as a ferrule and could only be fired after its removal. Not so the Remington-Thomas. That carried a screw-on hollow metal ferrule, the barrel hole being closed by a piece of cork carefully fitted for size and held by friction. While the makers recommended removing the ferrule, the gun could be fired safely with it still in position. One of the things Waco had done while using the gun for target practice was to re-fit the cork plug shot out by Hockley and paint it the same colour as the ferrule. Small wonder the two men failed to recognise the danger until too late.

Propelled by gasses caused from igniting the combustible cartridge's powder charge, the bullet passed along the gun's barrel, carried out the cork plug and ranged up to catch Tarrick in the mouth. Shock twisted the man's face and he staggered backwards. While his Colt bellowed, its barrel no longer lined at Waco and the bullet missed to ricochet from the corner of the safe.

Surprise caused Haver to swivel his head in Waco's direction as the cane-gun revealed its true purpose. In doing so he allowed the Derringer to waver slightly out of line.

Instantly Dusty thrust back his chair, sending it skidding across the room, but he did not rise. Instead he hurled himself forward and down through the desk's leg-hole. Never had he been more grateful for wearing his Colts in cross-draw holsters than at that moment. Drawing either gun from a butt-to-the-rear holster in the cramped confines through which he passed would have been almost an impossibility. While difficult, he managed to slide the left side Colt out with his right hand as he passed beneath the desk.

When he emerged at the other side, he came out shooting. Not just shooting but getting off his shots in the fastest possible manner when using a single-action revolver. Although some firearms' manufacturers produced double-action weapons, allowing the hammer to be cocked by pressure on the trigger, the Colt company preferred the more rugged and less complicated single-action for the majority of their products. While this allowed the weapon to operate with a minimum of working parts, an advantage in an age when repairs must be carried out by a local gun-smith who owned few tools, it meant the hammer needed manually cocking before it fired.

To overcome this slight disadvantage, Western gun-fighters had developed the art of fanning the hammer. True very few of them achieved success using such a method, but there was no quicker way of getting off shots from a single-action revolver. And in really skilled hands it could be surprisingly accurate at short range.

Dusty possessed that kind of skill. As he came into view, his right elbow rammed tight against his side to help control the gun. Whipping across his left hand, he forced over the hammer with its heel. Already his right forefinger held back the trigger, so the hammer did not engage and slammed down upon the waiting percussion cap on being released.

Still sliding forward, Dusty continued to fan the hammer as fast as he could circle his left hand around and repeat the cycle of operation. He shot fast for a definite purpose, to save his own life. While Waco had given him a chance and his unexpected action kept him out of Haver's line of fire, he did not know how quickly the man would recover from the surprise and change the Remington's aim. Black powder burned into a thick cloud of propellant gas and Dusty hoped to churn enough of it out to make him an uncertain target even if the bullets missed.

Only they did not miss. Three times in very quick succession lead ripped up into Haver's body and hurled him backwards. Nor did they strike a moment too soon. Already the wicked little hide-out gun had started to slant down and flame sparked from the upper of its superimposed twin barrels. Dusty heard a 'whomp!' at the side of his head as the Derringer's bullet churned into the floor alongside him. Then Haver toppled over backwards, crashing down some distance from where he had been standing.

Dropping the cane as soon as it had served his needs, Waco

bent and caught hold of his left hand Colt's butt. While he used his right hand and knew by the feel that it held the wrong gun, he wasted no time in changing. Instead he sent the holster flipping from the Colt and whirled in time to see Haver go down. Then the youngster swung towards Tarrick.

Blood gushing from his mouth, the man hung against the front wall. He had dropped his gun on being hit and showed no signs of further resistance. Even as Waco moved forward, shock and pain slid Tarrick unconscious to the floor. At the same moment Waco heard Dusty let out a pain-filled curse.

"Did he get you?" the youngster asked in concern, swinging towards the small Texan.

"No. I spiked a splinter into my butt-end as I slid through," Dusty replied and rose to his feet. "Thanks, boy. You handled that just right."

"I was scared as hell I'd not get away with it."

"The day you're scared, I'll vote Republican," Dusty said and rubbed his rump, then drew free the long splinter. "It was close, boy. If I never have a closer one, I'll be happy."

"And me."

"You'd best get the doctor for that jasper you shot. I'll do what I can for him until you get back."

Knowing that the need might arise for reaching some place in town faster than on foot, Dusty had arranged that one of the deputies kept his horse out back of the building while on watch. Collecting his waiting paint, Waco rode out of town and headed for the sports area. There he found and notified the doctor who left immediately. Using his initiative, the youngster next located the sheriff and told what happened. Like the doctor, Bracker returned to the marshal's office.

"There's not much chance for him, Captain Fog," the doctor stated after examining Tarrick. "The bullet's torn his tongue apart; even if I can stop the bleeding, he won't be able to eat."

"That's what I figured," Dusty replied.

"And that other man, Smith's companion, died late last night."

"So you told us."

"Doesn't it mean anything to you, Captain?" the doctor demanded.

"If you mean, am I sorry, the answer's 'yes'," Dusty answered quietly. "But I'd do it again under the same conditions. This's a rough country, doctor. There's not much law in it. Maybe the time'll come when a man doesn't need to strap on a gun in a morning, but until it comes I'll do what I have to do."

"Those two men died—," the doctor began.

"It was their own choosing," Dusty pointed out. "If that feller with Smith hadn't been stopped, he'd've killed one of us. Those two here might have just left Waco and me in a cell when they took Smith and pulled out; but it was a chance I couldn't take."

"Captain Fog did what he had to do, doctor," Bracker put in. "Sure he had to do some killing, but this territory's a mite safer for honest folks because of it."

"Let's get this feller into a cell," Dusty suggested, wanting the discussion over. "It'll be easier for him than lying on the floor."

The doctor nodded. While he might be new to the West, he had heard of other trail-end towns. Suddenly he realised that the one reason Mulrooney did not see the wild times of the other towns was because of Dusty's handling. So he chopped off his intention of continuing to raise the moral issues of the affair and supervised the removal of the wounded man.

"Now what happened, Dusty?" asked the sheriff once Tarrick was lying on a bunk in one of the cells.

"It's like we figured, Tom. Tricky Dick doesn't know where the money is."

"How'd you know that?" Waco inquired.

"Why else would he send two of his men here to get Smith out?" Dusty asked.

"But Smith didn't know the money'd gone," the youngster objected.

"He didn't," Dusty agreed.

"Then how'd he be able to find it?'

"That's a right smart question," Bracker put in.

"He's an idea where Stayley could have hid it," Dusty replied.

"Look, Dusty," Waco said slowly. "I might be hell with the gals—."

"You sure are," grinned Dusty.

"But I'm not smart like you," the youngster continued, ignoring the interruption. "So just sort of explain things real slow, easy and in itty-bitty words that dumb lil ole me can understand."

"It's easy enough. Stayley couldn't say to the others 'Wait here while I sneak off secret-like and hide the money.' And there's a limit to how many times he could find excuses to leave them before they got suspicious. I'd say three or four at the outside. Smith knows those places and a search around them'd likely turn up the money."

"That figures," Bracker admitted. "Only why doesn't Tricky Dick just follow their line instead of trying to pry Smith loose?"

"It's near on fifty miles to Newton, by the line those three'd take and none of it easy trailing country, or they don't know their business," Dusty guessed. "Also there'll be posses out hunting for them. Nope, Tricky Dick's best bet is to get Smith out, learn where Stayley could've hid the money and then pick it up."

"Maybe one of them pair's Tricky Dick," Waco suggested.

"Not if the description I've got's anywhere near right," Bracker answered. "He's a middle-sized jasper, looks like a swish, but he's tougher than any no-bullfighter* when the chips go down."

"He'd have to be to handle fellers like Stayley and those two," Dusty commented. "Thing now is, will he send some more of his boys, or try himself the next time?"

"You reckon he'll make another go at freeing Smith?" Bracker asked.

"Likely," Dusty replied. "He's taken so much trouble that he'll have to go through with it to show the rest of his bunch he's still the big man."

"Could be they'll fight shy of trying and expect him to do it," Bracker said. "Which means Tricky Dick'll be handling the next try hisself."

"Let's hope he does," Dusty answered. "Maybe we can nail his hide to the wall with Smith for the bait."

"Wells Fargo're going to want Smith pretty bad," Bracker pointed out.

"Could be," Dusty admitted. "Only I reckon we'll have something to say about that."

*Swish, no-bullfighter : effeminate.

9

Just a Half-Smart Lil Texas Boy

There was a heated scene in the marshal's office when the two real Wells Fargo special investigators finally reached Mulrooney. Once again the Cansole gang had cut the telegraph wires to prevent word of their exploits being passed ahead of them. Even after the investigators had been found in the men's room at the whistle-stop and freed, a considerable delay had ensued before contact could be made with the outside world. Travelling up by a special train sent out for them, the two men arrived at Mulrooney expecting the worst to have happened.

Smarting under the indignity at having been tricked into entering the room at the whistle-stop, clubbed insensible then left bound and gagged, they showed relief on learning that the rescue bid had failed. Their pleasure ended when Dusty flatly refused to turn Smith into their tender care. All he would do was allow them to interrogate the prisoner in his presence and he used the myth of the *Kansas City Intelligencer* reporter's presence to damp down any tendencies to take revenge for their mishaps.

"Damn it, marshal!" one of the investigators growled, when Smith continued to pretend innocence. "We're getting nowhere with him. If I can just—."

"Not in my jail," Dusty interrupted firmly.

"Then turn him over to us!"

"I reckon he'd be safer here—and if it comes to a point, you've nothing to prove he was mixed up in the hold-up. So I'm holding him for the attempted murder of a deputy marshal."

Anger glowed in the investigator's eyes, but a suggestion of another reason for Dusty's refusal died unsaid. Small he might be, but Dusty Fog stood in no man's shadow when it came to salty toughness. He would take the strongest objection to a suggestion that he might be holding Smith in the hope of laying hands on the hold-up money for his own use.

"J.B. Hume won't like this when he hears, marshal," the investigator contented himself with saying.

"Tell him to take it up with me," Bracker put in, having stayed at the office to witness the interview. "I'm backing Cap'n Fog all the way."

In the face of such opposition the Wells Fargo men realised they could do nothing. So they stamped indignantly from the office and headed for their Mulrooney depot to telegraph James B. Hume, the company's able chief of detectives. An answer came back promptly, but as a complete surprise. Hume ordered his men to give the local law every co-operation and to leave Smith in the marshal's hands. Grudgingly the pair returned to tell Dusty the news, little guessing that he had communicated his plans for using Smith as bait to Hume before they arrived.

With that matter attended to, Dusty started to plan for foiling further efforts by Cansole to rescue the prisoner. Even should no attempt be made, Dusty felt that Smith might respond to hints of being double-crossed by helping the law find the hold-up loot.

So, on Monday morning, Smith went before the local judge who ordered he be held in custody for a week to allow a full investigation into the attempted murder of a deputy town marshal. That decision came about as a result of a consultation with Dusty. While it might not be in accordance with the strict letter of the law, both the small Texan and the judge felt it would be worthwhile. So Smith found himself faced with another seven days in the Mulrooney jail. During that time both he and Dusty hoped that Cansole would try again.

Preparing for the attempt, should it come, Dusty warned his staff to remain constantly alert for tricks and to watch everybody who tried to make contact with Smith. Not that Dusty thought Smith would be stupid enough to part with his information before being rescued. The outlaw had sense enough to know that once Cansole learned where to look for the money, he need no longer waste time, or risk losing more men, in further rescue bids.

Despite the threat of other jail-breaking attempts, the normal routine of the office had to go on. Towards noon on Monday the man who had bought Buffalo Kate's Brownton saloon arrived in Mulrooney, backed by several hard-cases, to take revenge on her for what he regarded as trickery. Only the arrival of Dusty and shotgun-armed deputies saved Kate. Being challenged by the vengeance-seeker, Dusty fought and killed him with duelling swords, the man making the mistake of believing such weapons offered him the best chance when dealing with a known gun-fighter.

Nothing further of note happened on Monday, except that the smouldering feud between Freddie Woods and Buffalo Kate received further fuel when the latter used information given by the former to hire a top-grade attraction to appear at the Buffalo Saloon and stole the majority of the trade.

Much as Dusty wanted to remain on hand around the jail, circumstances on Tuesday prevented him from doing so. Various civic dignitaries organised a banquet for the cattle-buyers, trail bosses and other important visitors. As segundo and trail boss of the great OD Connected, Dusty received an invitation to attend. So did Mark Counter, going along to represent his father's R Over C spread and other Texas Big Bend interests.

It was Frank Derringer's night off watch. Although he offered to help out, Dusty felt the need would not arise. Called to deal with a disturbance at the Fair Lady—a gandy-dancer claimed his pocket was picked while he watched a game of strip-poker between Babsy and three other girls—the Kid and Big Sarah left Waco in charge of the office. On their return, Waco decided to make the rounds. From the start, the youngster had showed such an affinity for peace officer work that the Kid did not hesitate to let him go alone.

Although considerable noise was coming from the Fair Lady, the rest of the town seemed peaceful enough. Then Waco heard the crack of a shot and a crash of breaking glass. Halting for a moment, he decided the sound came from the Buffalo Saloon and headed in that direction on the run.

While he might be conscious that he was handling his first lone-hand work since becoming a deputy, Waco did not forget the lessons Dusty had taught him. Instead of dashing straight into the saloon, he halted on the sidewalk and looked through one of the big front windows. A hold-up might be in progress, or a shoot-out between two enemies, either of which offered con-siderable danger to a peace officer who burst in unprepared to deal with them.

81

Nothing so dramatic met his gaze, although what he saw did not fill him with joy. The strip-poker game at the Fair Lady had sucked in most of the trade, as Freddie hoped when she organised it, but the Buffalo had managed to draw some custom. Not that much drinking, gambling or other business was being done, for employees and customers alike sat and stood in attitudes of strained immobility staring at the two men who monopolized the front of the long bar.

Waco sucked in a deep breath as he looked at the men. Each equalled his height, one lean, the other heavier. From their smoke-blackened and blood-stiff buckskin clothing, the sheathed knives at their belts and moccasin-covered feet, he took them to be buffalo-hunters. Unshaven, long-haired and dirty, they most likely were just back from a hunt. Probably they had sold their hides and started a celebration before taking a bath, hair-cut, shave and change of clothes. By all appearances, they carried enough whiskey internally to feel festive—and, like cowhands, they found their fun by shooting off guns.

Even as Waco watched, the heavier of the pair cut loose with a revolver shot that burst a bottle on the table before a scared-looking town dweller. Not to be out-done, the second hunter shattered a beer schooner. Buffalo Kate, looking angry and concerned, stood on the stairs leading to the first floor rooms. Unless the youngster missed his guess, she aimed to try to stop the men. Only he could not see them taking orders from a woman.

In any case, it was his duty as a deputy town marshal to go in and keep the peace. So he must enter and do something; the problem being what to do. Maybe the pair did not intend to hurt anybody, and cold sober could shoot accurately enough, but they had drunk sufficient to become unsteady. At any moment one of them might waver in his aim, putting the bullet into human flesh, not an inanimate object. Even if it did not happen, the reckless shooting had to be stopped. Let word once go around that buffalo-hunters had shot up a saloon unchecked and some cowhand was certain sure to try to uphold the honour of his profession by out-doing them. Sooner or later somebody would be hurt.

Darting a glance towards the marshal's office, Waco could see no sign of the Kid. While not afraid for his own sake, the youngster wished he had a more experienced man along to guide him. Knowing how easily the carefully built reputation Dusty had created might be spoiled, he did not wish to do the wrong thing. A glaring error of judgement on his part might easily ruin all Dusty's good work. Yet, on the final analysis, he felt that Dusty would rather have him do something and be wrong rather than nothing, permitting a breach of the peace.

"Now was I a real smart Kansas lawman, I'd quick enough let windows in their bellies from the street and then go in to tell 'em to quit," Waco mused as he walked towards the batwing doors. "Trouble being I'm just a half-smart lil Texas boy. So I'll have to do it the hard way."

"Yahoo!" whooped the heavier man as Waco reached the doors. "I'm as tough as a hickory log. I can dive deeper and come up dryer than any man on the Great Plains."

Sucking in a deep breath, Waco pushed open the doors and stepped through. Every eye in the room turned his way and a slight air of expectancy ran through all but the two trouble-makers. They swivelled whiskey-wild faces his direction, taking in his empty hands and the badge on his vest.

"You wanting something, boy?" demanded the lean jasper, twirling his Colt in a manner which showed liquor had not fumbled his reflexes to any great extent.

"Now you-all wouldn't be fixing to spoil our fun, would you?" his companion continued, lining a Starr Army revolver in Waco's direction with disconcerting steadiness of hand. "Me 'n' Eli here wouldn't care for that."

Catching Buffalo Kate's eye, the bartender waited for a signal to take a hand. The woman hesitated, not sure what to do for the best. Since her arrival in Mulrooney, she had developed the greatest respect for all the local law officers. If possible she wanted to help for that reason, but another one sprang to mind. She knew Dusty, Mark and the Kid regarded Waco as their protege and like a favourite younger brother. If he should be shot down, the men who did it were sure to pay. Yet that could easily start bad trouble between the cowhands and buffalo-hunters, for both factions would side with their own.

Just as Kate prepared to signal to the bartender, she caught Waco's eye and the youngster shook his head. Such was her faith in the marshal's office that she refrained from passing a sign for her bartender to gather up the sawed-off ten gauge from under the counter. As the shotgun lay at the far end of the shelf, the bartender let out a faint sigh of relief.

"All I came in for's a drink," Waco assured the men, walking forward.

Used to the normal run of Kansas lawmen, who would have entered behind a lined shotgun—provided they did not send in two loads of buckshot first—the buffalo-hunters accepted his explanation. Yet neither relaxed to any great extent, which precluded any chance of drawing and covering them, even if doing so would solve the problem.

"You look kind of young to be wearing that badge," Eli commented.

"The marshal's my uncle," Waco explained with a disarming grin.

"So he figured the town might's well pay and feed you 'stead of him, huh?" asked the second man, lowering the Starr.

"Don't talk it out loud," Waco said urgently. "The tax-payers might hear. Say, that was mighty slick shooting I saw you doing —Near on as slick as I've ever seen."

"He reckons he's seed better'n us, Zeb," Eli growled.

"Maybe he'd like to see some more," the other buffalo-hunter replied.

"Now what I calls shooting's what I've seen Uncle Dusty do," Waco put in before the men could decide what action to take. "Why I've seen him stand like where I am now and shoot a whiskey bottle as it slid along the bar top. Now *that's* what I call shooting."

"Yeah," said Zeb, sounding a might subdued.

"There's not many can do it," Waco went on. "It's too hard for most."

"Hah! It ain't all that hard," snorted Eli. "Least-wise not for buffalo-hunting gents like us."

"I've seen Uncle Dusty hit five out of six. Now there's real lead-slinging."

"G'wan!" Zeb snorted. "He missed one, didn't he?"

"I've never seen it beat," Waco replied.

"By cracky, you will this time!" Eli yelped and swung towards the bartender. "You slide a whiskey bottle down there, feller."

Directing a glance at his boss, the bartender saw her nod. While Kate did not know what Waco was planning, she guessed more than mere boasting lay behind his words. So she went along with him, wondering if he hoped the sound of the shooting would bring Dusty and the others to help deal with the men.

"Ready?" the bartender asked, taking one of the empty bottles from beneath the counter.

"Go to it," Waco replied and looked at the men. "You have to let it get right to the end afore you cut loose."

Whatever his motive, Kate realised that Waco aimed to minimize the damage to her property. If the men allowed the bottle to reach the end of the bar before shooting, provided they came anywhere near close to their target, the bullet would end its flight harmlessly in the building's wall. The outer timbers were of sufficient thickness to prevent a revolver bullet bursting through. So she moved slowly down the stairs, watching every action the trio made.

The bartender sent the bottle sliding along the polished top of the counter with a deft flick of his wrist. Bringing up his Starr, Zeb fired and missed, the bottle coming to a halt on the edge of the counter. However Eli had been watching Waco all the time and presented no opportunity for him to make a move.

"Missed," grinned the youngster.

"Dang it, so did your uncle!" Zeb replied hotly.

"Skim another down and leave me try a try," Eli suggested.

Puzzled by Waco's actions, the bartender still felt no inclination to make a move himself. If Kate gave him the sign he would, but until then he felt content to go along with the young Texan's wishes.

Like Zeb, Eli discovered that shooting a sliding bottle proved a tricky proposition.

"Dag-nab it!" the lean hunter wailed as the bottle stopped unbroken by his bullet. "That danged mirror threw light back into my eyes. Maybe I ought to do something about it."

"Busting it'd sure be a heap easier than hitting that bottle," Waco agreed, determined to prevent such an expensive piece of damage.

Slowly Eli lowered the Colt from pointing at the mirror. The young deputy's words had carried all around the room. So if Eli did throw lead into the mirror, everybody would reckon it was because he lacked the skill to hit the bottle. Conscious that he upheld the honour and dignity of the buffalo-hunting fraternity, Eli could not allow such a thing to happen.

"Damn it, send her along again!" he growled.

Once more the bottle made its glide along the counter.

85

Although both men fired, no shattering of glass gladdened their ears.

"Danged if you didn't put me aim off, partner," Zeb said.

"I never figured you'd blast off in my ear just as I pressed the trigger," Eli protested. "You leave me do it next time."

If Waco had hoped to cause a rift between the two men, he failed. The misses merely increased their desire to shatter that hateful bottle. Eli tried again with no better result. Then Zeb made another attempt, shooting twice and bursting the bottle with the second bullet.

"Done it!" he whooped.

"Lemme have one, barkeep!" yelled Eli, not wishing to be out-done.

More by luck than skilled aim Eli managed to shatter the bottle, although it had almost come to a stop when he hit it. A point which Waco immediately brought out in a loud tone.

"Uncle Dusty hits them at full slide," he announced. "Not when they've just about stood still."

"Yeah?" snorted Eli. "Well as soon as I've reloaded, I'll show you how its done."

"Just let me fill my old Starr's chamber," Zeb went on. "Then I'll hit six outa six. I was just getting the range."

"You mean you gents're empty?" asked Waco with deceptive mildness.

"Sure am, boy," agreed Eli.

"And me," confirmed Zeb.

Then both of them froze, staring into the barrels of the matched Army Colts which flashed from Waco's holsters and lined on them.

"Now you just put up your guns and we'll take us a walk down to the jailhouse."

"What—!" Eli squalled.

"Why you—!" Zeb bellowed.

But they stood very still, for neither had drunk enough to dull their perceptions at such a moment. The speed with which Waco drew, and the way he thumb-cocked the hammers and pressed back the triggers *after* the barrels had left leather and slanted away from him, did not go unnoticed by the men. Faced by such mastery, even with a fair load of whiskey in them, they knew better than to make any foolish moves.

"By cracky, boys," Buffalo Kate said, coming forward. "He

sure out-foxed you."

Then the humour of the situation struck the crowd. They suddenly realised that the youngster's actions since entering the saloon had been for a purpose. Nor did the difference between his method of disarming the pair and that which most Kansas lawmen would have employed go unnoticed. A man started to laugh and others took it up. All the tension went from the crowd as they howled their mirth. Slowly the baffled anger faded from the faces of Eli and Zeb, then they too joined in the laughter as heartily as anybody.

"Everything all right, Waco?" asked the Kid, walking in with his Winchester cradled over the crook of his right arm.

"I reckon so," the youngster replied. "These gents've just been showing me some right fancy shooting and now they're fixing to show me how fancy they are at sweeping up broken glass."

"How's that?" Eli asked, watching Waco's Colts return to leather.

"I figure you owe it to Miss Kate," the youngster told him. "Busting bottles all over the place."

"Which same it'd be easier than spending a night in the pokey," the Kid went on.

"I'll be damned if I believe anybody could hit a bottle at full slide," Zeb stated indignantly.

A grin twisted Waco's lips as he faced the bar. "Skip one along, friend."

Obediently the bartender picked up a bottle and sent it along at, if anything, a faster pace than the others. Waco's right hand dipped and rose, the room's lights glinted dully on blued steel, then his Colt roared from waist high. Glass flew as the bottle disintegrated in full motion and a concerted gasp passed around the room. Twirling the Colt into leather in almost a continuation of the draw and shot, he looked at the men.

"I'd do the other five, but the tax-payers buy fodder for my gun and'd rawhide me for wasting 'em," he said. "Miss Kate, set these gents a drink up on me and then hand them a brush each."

"Now there's a lawman I could get to like," grinned Zeb. "I heard this was a straight town, Kate—and it's true."

"You the best hand with a gun in the marshal's office, friend?" Eli asked, dropping the over-familiar condescension and 'boy'.

"There're two better than me," Waco replied.

"In that case, I'm leaving my gun empty," the lean buffalo-hunter stated. "Hand me a drink, then watch me go to sweeping."

"What'll Dusty say about me letting them do all that shooting?" Waco asked as he left the saloon with the Kid.

"That you did just right. Any other way and you'd've had to salt lead into that pair of hide-hunters."

"So I figured. Maybe I should've jumped them sooner."

"You did it just right," grinned the Kid. "Now stop fishing for compliments and let's get back to the office."

10

You're Not What I'd Call Welcome

Dusty confirmed the Kid's summing-up of Waco's actions when told on Wednesday morning and praised the youngster for the shrewd manner in which he had handled a tricky situation. So for the first time Waco felt himself capable of holding down his full end of the office's work.

While the youngster was learning fast and gaining confidence with each day, he had yet to come into conflict with the commission of a crime. Due to Dusty's policy of having a 'welcome committee' awaiting the arrival of every train and stage-coach, weeding out undesirables, the word went out that Mulrooney was bad medicine for petty criminals. None of the paying visitors who went broke regarded it as a fault of the town, for they received fairer treatment than in other such places along the railroad.

One of the girls employed in Lily Gouch's house stole a client's wallet during the transaction of business. However Lily, realising that she might never find another town which allowed her to operate without paying substantial bribes to various civic authorities, acted fast. In addition to returning the wallet, contents intact, to its owner, she gave the thief a beating calculated to make her fight shy of the touch of leather between her fingers for life. The other girls took the hint and there were no further incidents of that nature in the house.

Under the peaceful air of Wednesday morning, the town

seethed with excitement. The feud between the Fair Lady and Buffalo saloons grew hotter, causing considerable interest among citizens and visitors alike. While the game of strip-poker had put the Fair Lady ahead, nobody expected Buffalo Kate to stand back and accept defeat mildly. Nor did she. When the Buffalo opened for business on Wednesday, the girls wore dresses cut considerably shorter than accepted as usual, even in saloons. Naturally such an attraction hauled in trade and the town waited eagerly to see how Freddie planned to top it.

"Did Babsy tell you anything, boy?" asked the Ysabel Kid as he stood with Waco and Frank Derringer watching the noon train pull in to the depot on Thursday. "I'd sure admire to lay a bet on it with Mark—if I could be sure of winning."

"She never told me a thing," the youngster grinned. "Like I told Mark, when he asked so he could bet against you."

"Damned if the office's not crawling with sharps," Derringer commented, then nodded towards the train. "Here they come."

"You're bossing this drive," the Kid answered. "Point her the way you want to go."

In addition to being the office's gambling authority, Derringer possessed another asset. Travelling around in search of high-stake games of chance, he had come to know many of the assorted petty criminals Dusty wished to deny access to Mulrooney. So the gambler always attended the arrival of trains or stagecoaches and put his knowledge to good use.

Slowly the train ground to a halt, its driver timing things so that the passenger cars stopped in front of where the deputies stood. In addition, the conductor locked the end doors of the two cars, forcing the passengers to come out in the middle where Derringer's party could look them over conveniently.

"Howdy," greeted the gambler-deputy, blocking the path of a soberly-dressed, respectable-looking man who stepped from the forward car. "Can you tell me what *persona non grata* means?"

For a moment recognition flickered on the man's face, then it assumed a bland, puzzled expression. "I'm afraid I don't understand."

"It means 'No thanks, we've enough of our own.'," Derringer explained, thumbing open his jacket to expose the badge on his vest. "In other words, Mr. Ketter, this town doesn't need you."

"Kett—," the man began in a tone ringing with righteous indignation.

"You're blocking the other passengers," Derringer interrupted. "So just step aside, let them out and then get back aboard. Try going West, Ketter. Maybe they're short on gold-brick salesmen and card-sharks out there, but we've got all we want."

"I still don't know what you mean," the man stated, then shrugged. "But I'll do what you want and lodge a complaint with your bondsmen later."

With that he started to turn and his right hand disappeared from Derringer's sight in front of his body. The gambler did not hesitate. Catching Ketter by the left shoulder, Derringer swung him around and drove the other fist hard into his belly. A purist student of pugilism might have claimed that the punch went home a mite low for sportsmanship, but Derringer did not regard the affair in the nature of a sporting contest.

Nor did Ketter, judging by the way he gasped and started to fold over. On the heels of the blow, Derringer slashed his other hand from the shoulder to the side of Ketter's jaw and sent him sprawling at the feet of a tall nun just about to step down from the next car.

"If you wasn't reaching for that hid-out stingy gun, I'll think about apologising, Ketter," Derringer remarked, then looked at the nun and felt an explanation to be in order. "I'm sorry, ma'am. It was only a harmless bit of funning."

"So it seems," the nun replied, glancing down at the groaning Ketter. "I suppose Sister Bridget and I are *persona grata*?"

"Yes ma'am," Derringer agreed, seeing a second nun behind the speaker. "I reckon you are. Let me just help this gent out of your way."

Bending over Ketter, the deputy took hold of his jacket lapels and hauled him erect. Before the gasping man could shake the dizziness from his head and think about revenge, Derringer thrust him to one side. Then Derringer turned and watched the two nuns step down. Looking at the first of the pair, he wondered what had made such a beautiful woman renounce the world and take the veil.

Despite the habit which she wore hiding her figure, the woman conveyed an impression that what lay underneath would take seconds from none of her sex. Her face, framed severely, had beauty of a sultry kind that could not be hidden. She spoke with a refined New England accent and moved gracefully.

Behind her came a slenderly-built novice, walking with head

bowed and apparently conscious of the vow of silence imposed by her order.

"Can you direct me to the convent, deputy?" the beautiful nun asked. "I'm the new mother superior and Sister Bridget is a novice accompanying me there."

"Take the ladies along to the convent, will you, Waco," Derringer said and the youngster moved forward with no great show of enthusiasm.

"We couldn't think of interrupting you, or taking your assistant from his duty," the nun objected, glancing at the badge Waco wore. "Heaven only knows how many bad characters might get into town without you being here to stop them. I suppose you meet every train like this?"

"Trains and stagecoaches both, ma'am," Waco told her, relieved that he did not have to attend to such a minor chore when somebody interesting might come off the cars.

"How very thorough. I'll sleep more peacefully in my bed knowing that Mulrooney has such an efficient police force. Come Sister Bridget."

"I'll have somebody fetch your gear along, ma'am," Waco promised.

"Thank you, but I assure you that I can manage," the nun replied and walked across to where the usual bunch of loafers had gathered by the depot.

Body hunched in pain, breathing hard, Ketter glared at his assailant and snarled, "I'll not forget this, Derringer. One day—."

"Sure, I'll wait for the day to come," Derringer answered. "Could be I just saved your worthless life. Look—."

Following the direction indicated by the deputy, Ketter saw something that almost scared him out of a year's growth. Unnoticed until that moment the Ysabel Kid was lounging in the background, his rifle hanging negligently in his right hand. The negligence was more apparent than real, especially when taken with the position of his right forefinger. No man of the Kid's proven rifle-savvy curled that particular digit through the triggerguard unless prepared to start shooting. Cold sweat sent a shiver through Ketter at the sight. Recognising the Kid, he realised what his fate would have been had he drawn the Colt Cloverleaf revolver from its concealed holster.

"You're getting old and careless, *hombre*," commented the Kid amiably. "And you're not what I'd call welcome here."

91

"To hell with you and this whole stinking town!" Ketter spat back and turned to reboard the train.

Turning when he saw he would not be needed to deal with Ketter, Waco looked at the two nuns. They stood with one of the loafers, the novice silent and head bowed as before, the mother superior pointing with a white, elegant hand towards some baggage a Negro porter was bringing out of the second car. Something puzzled the youngster, a small thought nagging at the back of his mind but unable to break out in full. Before he could take time to mull over the matter, Derringer sent him to intercept a man and woman who the conductor suggested made a speciality of the old 'badger' game.

The couple, having seen Ketter's greeting, alighted on the other side of the car. Going over the platform, Waco jumped down and followed them.

"You won't like it here, even if we'd let you stop," he said.

Turning, the big, bulky man eyed the youngster from head to toe. Dressed in Eastern fashion, he did not wear a gun but looked a powerful bruiser with big, hard-knuckled hands.

"What's that?" the woman asked.

"The 'badger' game's mighty risky any place west of Chicago, ma'am," Waco replied. "Was I you, I'd head back to the Windy City."

"I don't get y—," the woman answered. She was a pretty thing, young and ideally suited for her part in the game.

"Gal in Hays was the last I knowed to try a 'badger' game," Waco told her. "Picked on a poor, half-smart Texas boy for it as her first one. Only when her husband come busting into the bedroom, he got his head blowed clean off—The feller they figured to 'badger' was John Wesley Hardin."

"Look, boy—," began the man, dropping their bags and advancing menacingly.

Then he came to a halt, staring in amazement at the Colt which flashed into Waco's hand. New out from the East, their knowledge of cowhands confined to one meeting in the comparatively civilized confines of Chicago, neither of the 'badger' pair had ever seen a real good Western gun-fighter draw. Like most folks who witnessed the phenomenon for the first time, the speed with which the gun appeared almost took their breath away.

"Mister, most cowhands're near on as fast as that and can hit what they aim at across the width of a bedroom," Waco warned, twirling away the Colt. "You take my advice and find some other town."

The man and woman exchanged worried glances. Operating the 'badger' game was simple. After the girl had lured a victim to her bedroom and disrobed, the man burst in on them. Claiming to be her husband, he accused the victim of alienating his wife's affections and demanded money to overlook the affair. While tough—he had fought in the prize-ring—the man realised that no amount of muscle could beat a heavy-calibre revolver. Smarter than her companion, the girl saw there would be little chance of operating in a town so efficiently policed, unless—

"You wouldn't—," she started.

"No, ma'am, I *wouldn't*," agreed Waco. "'Cause I'm a noble, true, honest lil Texas boy; and cause the marshal'd beat my pumpkin head shoulder-level if I let you bribe me to watch over you."

Deep rumbles came from the man, but the woman gave a philosophical shrug. "Thanks for the warning."

"Happen you don't take it, ma'am," Waco replied. "You'll wish you had."

Noting the underlying hardness in the youngster's voice, the woman nodded and told her companion to return to the train. While the man picked up his bags, Waco saw the two nuns and their helper come around the rear of the train. Holding the skirts of her habit up, the mother superior picked a dainty way over the rails on stylish shoes. As she saw Waco, she let the skirts drop with becoming modesty and flashed him a smile.

"Still doing your duty, deputy," she said.

"Yes, ma'am," he replied and then gave his attention to the 'badger' pair as they walked by him towards the train. By the time they had boarded the car, the nuns had passed out of sight between two buildings.

"And there's another good piece of work well done," Derringer commented as the train pulled out. "Even if I do say so myself."

"Let's take a look in on the Fair Lady as we go back," Waco suggested. "Maybe the gals'll be wearing their new outfits."

"And if they're not, you'll likely get a chance to talk to Babsy," the Kid grinned. "Chasing gals's all some of you fellers think about."

"Wasn't you ever young yourself, Lon?" asked Derringer as

they directed their feet towards the saloon.

"All them danged Injuns do for courting's steal hosses to give to the gal's pappy," Waco sniffed. "I reckon our way's a whole heap better."

"Stealing hosses's a whole mess of fun, boy," the Kid stated.

"Not as much fun as finding out that the gal's got no hair on her chest," Waco said without thinking and could have cheerfully bitten off his tongue.

"So *that's* what you did that night," Derringer gasped.

"For shame," the Kid went on. "And me thinking you'd learned some good ways since knowing me."

Waco's reply was blistering, profane and nothing to do with the subject of how he spent his night off watch. By the time he finished, they had reached the Fair Lady and he led the way inside.

If the deputies hoped to learn Freddie's plan to counter Buffalo Kate's attraction, they met disappointment. Being remarkably shrewd, the lady saloonkeeper did not intend to disclose her answer so early that her rival could defeat it. So the few girls present wore their normal dresses.

So far the only customers were a few townsmen and a quartet of younger visitors. The latter wore low-heeled, heavy boots and bib-overalls, which meant they did not belong to cowhand, buffalo-hunter or railroad trades. Looking at them, Waco concluded that they must be from the near-by sod-busting homesteads. Despite the fact that all they drank was beer, the quartet were entertaining all the girls.

"Hi," Waco greeted Vera, second of the barmaids. "Where's Babsy?"

"Trying on the new dress the boss'll have us wearing tonight, deputy," one of the girls called. "And is it something?"

"You'll get something if you blab your fool mouth off about it," Vera warned grimly. "What's it to be, gents?"

"You're buying, boy," Derringer stated.

"Am I?" Waco asked.

"You are happen you want me and Frank to forget about them hairs on the chest," the Kid told him.

"Damned if I shouldn't make you pair leave town!" Waco snorted. "Three beers and take something for yourself, Miss Vera."

"Just what's Miss Freddie fixing up back there, Vera gal?" the

94

Kid inquired after she served the drinks.

"Wait and see," the barmaid replied with a grin. "It'll make that Buffalo bunch sit back on their heels and wish they'd stopped back in Brownton."

Before any further attempt could be made by the interested trio to discover the secret, the Fair Lady received more customers. Half a dozen cowhands trooped in. From their fresh-bathed and barbered appearance, taken with the fact that all wore new clothes, they had only recently received their pay. No cowhand with money in his pocket ever wasted time in looking for a place to spend it. Nor did he want to spend it all on himself. The six cowhands came to the Fair Lady looking for drinks, fun and female company.

"Set up drinks, ma'am," ordered one of the party, hauling a wad of money from his pocket. "You gents from the marshal's office take something?"

"Just the one," Derringer replied. "The marshal'd slap a fine on us happen he caught us drinking."

"We wouldn't want to make lawmen bust the law," the cowhand grinned and looked along the bar. "Reckon you've any gals who'd take a drink with a bunch of thirsty Texas gents, ma'am?"

"Open up some wine if they do, ma'am," another cowhand went on. "They do say beer makes a gal fat."

"Let's keep it friendly, boys," Derringer said quietly, moving along the bar as one of the young farmers slammed down his beer schooner.

"You Texas boys seen the jail-house?" the Kid asked, facing the cowhands.

"Can't miss it, which same I've seen as good back to home," one of them answered.

"It's big and roomy," the Kid continued. "Trouble being they made the backhouse a mite small, so the marshal's having another built. He was just saying to me this morning how we ought to find somebody to dig the hole. Him and the judge allow to use the next bunch we bring in for making a fuss to dig it."

"The last thing we want's fuss," stated the leader of the cowhands.

However the girls drifted along the bar and joined the new-comers. Laughter rang out, along with squeals of pleasure as Vera decanted wine and other drinks that their previous companions could not afford.

"Blasted cowhands!" one of the young nesters spat out.

"You can't even buy a drink when they're here," another continued bitterly. "Let's try the Wooden Spoon, they don't have gals in there."

"It must be rough on the local kids," Derringer commented as the deputies watched the nesters stamp out of the saloon. "They come to town, but don't make the kind of money to compete with the cowhands, buffalo-hunters and railroad hands who drift in."

None of the trio had noticed Freddie enter from the rear. Coming up, she saw the nesters leave and heard Derringers' wry comment.

"What's the answer, Frank?" she asked.

"Huh?" he grunted, turning.

"To their problem. We have to keep our prices high to cover breakages and other overheads, like running through the winter when there're no trail-hands, buffalo-hunters or railroad construction gangs in. Or those who are have no money. So we go as high as the traffic will stand and the local boys are cut out because they can't afford it."

"Which must set in their craw something fierce at times," Derringer agreed. "Like just now."

"The girls shouldn't've walked away like they did," Freddie admitted. "But don't forget they're paid to entertain the customers, with bonuses for the amount spent. That means they go to those who can pay most. Mercenary, but understandable I suppose."

"Sure."

"Then what do I do, Frank?" Freddie insisted. "Stop the locals coming in during the trail season? That's not practical, or good business. They'll be around all through the winter. Let them pay less for their drinks than the visitors? Fine, until some visitor notices that I'm doing it. Have separate rooms, or a part of town, just for locals? It's been tried without much success in other places, or so I've heard. What *is* the answer, Frank?"

"You've got me," he admitted. "Human nature being what it is, whichever way you go, it'll be wrong for sure."

Freddie looked at the gambler with a smile. "You're either a cynic or a philosopher, Frank, but I don't know which."

"You tell me what they mean, and I'll right smart tell you which, ma'am," Waco put in. "Say, where-at's Babsy?"

"She'll be out when she's changed," Freddie promised and went on just a touch too innocently. "Have you been in the Buffalo today?"

"Nope," Derringer answered. "And if I had, I wouldn't say what I'd seen. One thing I'm not doing's getting mixed between you and Kate."

"You don't think I care what that fat trollop does, do you?" Freddie snorted, sounding as if she meant it.

"All I know is that coming between you two'd be worse than standing on a log between two bobcats," Derringer grinned.

"Which same you'll wish you was on that log happen Dusty has to come looking for us," the Kid remarked, setting down an empty glass. "Let's go and see what the boss man has for us to do."

"Knowing him," Waco replied. "It'll be something for certain sure."

II

It Goes with Wearing the Badge

"Well, what do you think?" Babsy asked, just a touch defiantly, as she twirled around in front of Waco to let him take in the full impact of the Fair Lady's answer to the Buffalo's challenge.

While aware that the rival saloon must be firmly put in its place, the little blonde felt a twinge of concern over how Waco might regard her appearance. The dress she wore ended just below the tops of her black stockings, exposing shapely legs to view, while the decollete was considerably more daring than anything so far achieved by the Buffalo's girls. Admiration flickered on the young deputy's face, for the dress set off Babsy's buxom figure to its best advantage.

"Whooee!" he said, reaching out and taking her by the arms. "Miss Kate'll have to go some to lick this, gal."

"Lay off!" Babsy ordered unconvincingly. "Give over."

They stood in a room at the rear of the Fair Lady, having met for a quick talk before starting their respective night's work.

Drawing Babsy to him, Waco bent and kissed her.

"If I wasn't on watch—," he breathed.

"And if I didn't have to work tonight, I'd say yes for sure," she replied. "Only Miss Freddie needs me to do some songs."

"It's surely hell," Waco said after kissing her again. "I'll have to get going, Babsy gal."

"You stay away from the Buffalo and that fat ginger-haired cow!" Babsy warned, opening the door to let him out.

"I wonder if she's got any hairs on her chest," Waco remarked.

"You just let me catch you trying to find out, that's all!" Babsy squealed and slammed the door in an attempt to hit him across the heels as he stepped into the night. Then she opened it again and peeked out. "Hey! Come back around ten and we'll take a walk."

"Why sure, honey. I'll take you to the livery barn to see the golden horse-shoe nail."

"Garn! A groom back home tried to show me it once."

"Maybe Ginger hasn't seen it," Waco grinned.

"She's old enough to have put it there," Babsy sniffed. "Ten o'clock."

"I'll be here, all being well," Waco promised and walked away as the door closed once more.

Still grinning, Waco strolled along the street. Take it any way, that Babsy was quite a gal. Then a frown wiped off the grin. Maybe Miss Freddie and Buffalo Kate were carrying their feud a mite too far with the abbreviations to their girls' costumes. While Freddie seemed to have gone the limit, Waco could not see Kate allowing the challenge to go unanswered. Waco wondered what further reductions the Buffalo girls could make to their clothing, if any, and whether the Fair Lady would be able to counter the measures.

Pleasant though the speculations might be, he shook them from his head and concentrated on the work for which the tax-paying citizens of Mulrooney had hired him. Derringer was supervising a high-stake poker game that night, while the Kid and Mark were keeping watch at the jail. As Dusty and Big Sarah both had other work, the youngster made the rounds alone. However, since handling the two hide-hunters at the Buffalo, he felt that he could cope with anything that came along.

Everything around town seemed peaceful enough, the newly-arrived cowhands enjoying themselves without running horse-races through the streets, or engaging in impromptu target practice. Maybe later things would liven up. Not that Waco cared if the pacific state continued. With almost a week's practical law-enforcement behind him, Waco had adopted the typical peace-officer's attitude. No longer did he hope for something exciting to happen, being content to stroll his rounds quietly and undisturbed.

As always the youngster did his work thoroughly. Passing Lily Gouch's establishment, he saw a few cow-horses standing hitched to the front fence, heard laughter and music from inside but did not enter. Lily ran a quiet, orderly disorderly house and the law saw no reason to interfere with it. So the youngster walked on, heading for the livery barn.

Always a tempting target for thieves, despite horse-stealing being a hanging offence, the barn received frequent visits by the patrolling deputies. So did the neighbouring freight outfit's warehouse, which also carried items to attract outlaws.

Coming towards the rear of the two buildings, Waco saw that a light was glowing in the freight outfit's first-floor office window. As usual the outside stairs up to the office were illuminated by a hanging lantern at their head. Walking between the two businesses' corrals, Waco saw a pair of men coming hurriedly down the stairs. Though the light, being behind them, threw their faces into deep shadow, he could see enough to realise they were neither clerks from the office, nor company drivers.

The one in the lead would be Waco's size and build, wearing a Stetson hat of some age and north-country style, a red and black check mackinaw jacket, levis pants hanging outside heavy, low-heeled boots, with a Ballard single-shot rifle in his right hand, the left gripping a bulging floursack. Shorter and slighter built, the second man wore a black wolf-skin coat that reached his knees, pants tucked into the same kind of boots as his companion's, a battered U.S. cavalry campaign hat without its insignia, and toted a long-barrelled, muzzle-loading shotgun.

Everything about the pair warned Waco that they meant trouble. So he moved forward ready to draw and shoot should the need arise. Even as he opened his mouth to yell out a challenge the two men saw him.

"Beat it!" hissed the taller and leapt for the darkness beyond the lamp's pool of light.

Without offering to raise the shotgun, fortunately for him,

the second man sprang with commendable speed after his companion.

"Hold it!" Waco yelled, right hand flowing down to draw its Colt as he lunged out from between the corrals. However the two men gave no sign of obeying the command.

One of the rules Dusty had emphasised from the start was that a gun must be used only as a last resort, not as a convenient means of halting a fleeing suspect. So Waco held his fire. If the pair had offered resistance, the youngster would have acted without hesitation; but he could not shoot down men who ran away.

Already the men were dashing through the shadows towards the end of the building. Colt in hand, Waco set off after them, running at an angle before the freight outfit's warehouse. Then he saw two figures appear at the office window, throwing up its lower section to look out. He recognised them as the outfit's clerk having met them both around town. With that thought in mind, he continued to run, ignoring the fact that each of the clerks held a revolver. Wanting to catch up with the fleeing pair, the youngster clean forgot that the darkness made him an indistinct, unidentifiable shape. He learned the mistake quickly enough.

"There he is, Willy!" screeched the chubby clerk Gus Schubert, pointing down at the running deputy.

Swinging up the Colt he held, Willy Wallenheim fired. Before Waco could realise his error of tactics and yell a warning, he heard the bullet cut through the air over his head. Glaring upwards, he saw Schubert also taking aim at him and wasted no time in trying to explain matters to the clerks. The previous Sunday, before Babsy and Ginger caused his return to the office, Waco had seen the two clerks shooting in a competition. Although they did not measure up to the exacting standards of a Western-trained gun-fighter, each had proved himself more than adequate at target shooting over sights. Enough for Waco to realise that he must take no chances with them.

Ahead rose the big horse-trough, filled with water and offering the kind of solid shelter his heart desired at that moment. With another bullet making its eerie 'splat!' sound as it winged by his head, Waco dived across the trough and landed in the welcome blackness beyond it. That he came down in an area left permanently wet and muddy did little to cool the anger he felt at the clerks' actions. From the darkness where the fleeing men had disappeared came the creaking of saddle leather as they mounted waiting horses.

"Hey!" yelled Waco, starting to rise.

Instantly Wallenheim's revolver cracked, water erupted from the surface of the trough and the bullet rapped on the side, its progress so slowed by the liquid contents that it could not break through. However the nearness of the bullet and the fact that Schubert had taken aim caused Waco to duck down faster than he came up. Under different conditions he could have dealt with the pair. Standing in front of the window, they offered a perfect target in its rectangle of light. Unfortunately they were on the side of the law and acting in ignorance. Otherwise Waco could have been throwing lead their way instead of taking cover. Flattened on the muddy ground, the fuming youngster heard the sound of hooves drumming away and knew the other two men had escaped. Then the sound of shouts reached his ears, followed by feet running in his direction.

Two familiar shapes appeared cautiously around the right hand corner of the building, while a third came into sight at the left.

"Law here!" yelled the Ysabel Kid. "Hold up on that shooting."

"One of 'em's behind the horse-trough!" Wallenheim shouted back in a voice pitched high with excitement.

Instantly Mark Counter and the Kid faced the required direction, Winchester and Colt aiming at the trough as they moved apart to offer a smaller target along with the problem of whom to shoot at first. At the other end of the building, Dusty Fog advanced watchfully to where he could see and shoot at the ear of the trough should that prove necessary.

"Come on out with your hands showing and empty!" Mark bellowed, wanting to hold their man's attention and keep him from noticing Dusty.

"I'm coming!" Waco shouted back. "Just make sure them two *loco boboes* up there don't shoot me in the head when I get up."

At any other time the youngster might have enjoyed the consternation his voice caused. He saw Mark and the Kid stiffen in their tracks and heard a startled gasp from the window. Looking up, he saw the clerks hurriedly jerk back into the room and started to rise.

"Is that you, boy?" Mark asked.

"You're expecting maybe the whole blasted Dick Dublin gang?" the furious youngster replied, standing erect. "God damn it. Them two son-of-a-bitching bastards were like to kill me and let the real owlhoots get clear away."

Before any more could be said, the office door flew open and the two clerks clattered down the stairs.

"Have you got him, Kid?" Schubert asking, brandishing his revolver in an alarming manner.

"We sure have," agreed the Kid. "And a right desperate villain he is."

Clearly the clerks had been hoping that their ears and eyes had played tricks on them from the window. Their eyes went to where Waco stood behind the trough and noticed Dusty coming up behind the youngster.

"It *is* you, Waco," Wallenheim gasped.

"I've knowed that all along," the youngster answered bitterly.

"We didn't know!" Wallenheim croaked, suddenly aware of how close he had come to making a terrible mistake. "You came running by just as we opened the window and we thought you must be one of the robbers."

"You ought to have yelled out who you were, boy," the Kid put in. "How'd these gents know who you might be?"

"Maybe you'd best tell us what happened," Mark said to the clerks, before Waco's spluttering fury could erupt into a reply.

"Two men came bursting in and robbed us!" Wallenheim answered, darting a nervous glance at the youngest deputy.

"One of them had a shotgun," Schubert went on. "There wasn't a thing we could do but open the safe and give them the money."

"They took three thousand dollars from the safe, our watches and wallets," Wallenheim continued. "Get after them."

"How?" the Kid asked quietly.

"How?" Schubert yelped. "They can't have gone far."

"They'd've gone a damned sight less if you hadn't—!" Waco started hotly, still standing by the trough and unaware that Dusty was coming towards him.

Stepping up behind the youngster, Dusty caught hold of his arm and chopped off the rest of his speech.

"Hush your mouth, boy," the small Texan ordered. "Let them do the talking."

"Damn it all, Dusty," Waco protested, "if they'd let me go

by, instead of throwing lead at me, I could've run them two down afore they reached their hosses."

"And likely got your fool head blowed off with the scatter," Dusty replied. "Could be they saved your life, boy."

"*They* saved *my* life!" the youngster spluttered. "All they did—."

"Was make a fool mistake," Dusty interrupted quietly. "Most folks do that once in a while. Even us Texans."

"They damned nigh killed me!"

"Don't you reckon they know that?"

"Huh?"

"Look at them, boy!" Dusty ordered. "They're both near on sick thinking what they might have done."

"I'm not dancing with joy myself," Waco growled.

"You've been shot at before, and likely will again if you keep on wearing a badge," Dusty told him. "Those boys've never before been in a tight like that. Standing on the wrong end of a scattergun for the first time's mighty unnerving and right likely to make a man think or act a mite foolish."

"Likely," the youngster agreed.

"It's certain, not just likely!" Dusty snapped. "I know how you feel, and'd probably feel the same had it happened to me. Only if you go in there, head down and pawing dirt, you'll make them forget every damned thing that'll help us hunt for those two yahoos."

"If they hadn't—."

"And if Babsy was a boy, you wouldn't give a damn whether she has hair on her chest or not."

"How the hell did you—."

"I'll tell you when you're older. Right now no amount of 'ifs' can change what's done. So we have to play the hand with the cards that're left. Wasting time thinking how you could've maybe run them down if you hadn't been stopped's no use. You did get stopped. So now we've got to work another way."

"So what do I do?" Waco asked.

"First thing is forget that they tossed lead at you," Dusty replied. "Mark it down to experience, boy. It goes with wearing the badge. Reckon you can do it?"

"I'll give it a whirl," the youngster promised, then grinned. "If I can go see Babsy later."

"Damned if you're not getting as bad as Lon and Mark,"

Dusty told him. "All right, do it and you can go off early."

"For a chance to see Babsy, I'd say I did all the shooting at myself," Waco stated. "Have you seen how Miss Freddie's got them gals dressed?"

"I've seen," Dusty answered. "Let's go talk to the clerks."

Something in the small Texan's voice and attitude warned Waco that he did not entirely approve of the Fair Lady's dress style. Waco wondered why, knowing that mere prudery was not the cause of the grim note in Dusty's voice. However he knew it was neither the time nor the place to raise the question.

Waco studied the two clerks' faces as he walked towards them with Dusty, reading the sick anxiety each showed. Taken with the distracted manner in which they glanced towards him while he spoke to Dusty, Waco began to understand his companion's insistence that he should overlook their actions. Worried by thoughts of what they might have done, the pair paid little attention to the Kid's questions. So Waco prepared to accept responsibility for their over-excited error.

"I—I'm real sorry that we shot at you, Waco," Wallenheim said.

"It was all my fault," the youngster replied. "I ought to have yelled out who I was when you opened the window."

"We could've killed you," Schubert continued.

"Shucks! I figured you was shooting to hold me down, not to hit me," Waco told him. "I didn't get hurt, so everything's fine."

In the face of the youngster's attitude, the clerks began to regain their confidence. The numb horror at discovering they had almost shot a peace officer wore off and they began to think rationally.

"Let's take a look in the office," Dusty said. "You come along, Waco. It's a slim chance, Lon, but get a lamp and see if there're any tracks. Mark, you'd best go back to the office. This could be a trick to get us away while they free Smith."

Going up to the office with the clerks and Waco, Dusty asked to be told all that happened.

"We were working on the books—," Schubert began.

"They came in through the door there—," Wallenheim started at the same moment.

"Suppose we let Gus tell it first," Dusty interrupted. "You listen, Willy, and see if you can think of anything he missed."

"Like I said," Schubert commenced. "We were working on the

books when the door opened. We thought it was the wrangler bringing up a can of beer. Only it was those two fellers. They'd got guns pointing at us, a shotgun and a rifle, and told us to hand over our wallets. We did it, marshal—."

"So would I, with a scattergun pointed at me," Dusty assured him. "You say they told you to hand over your wallets first?"

"Yeah. Then they took our watches and I thought they'd leave. Only the big one saw the safe door open—."

"You had the safe open?" Waco put in.

"Of course," Schubert answered. "How else could we check the money against the ledgers?"

"What'd they do then?" Dusty asked.

"The one with the shotgun kept us covered and the other picked up a flour-sack that we use for a door mat. He put the money from the safe in it, along with our wallets and watches. Then they made us lie face down on the floor and left. As soon as we thought it'd be safe, we got up, grabbed the guns from the desk and went over to the window."

"What'd they look like?" Dusty inquired before the clerks could start brooding on what had followed their opening the window.

"It's hard to say. They wore bandanas over their faces and their hats covered their hair."

"About how tall were they?"

"The one with the rifle was about Waco's size and the other closer to mine."

"Anything you can tell us that Gus missed, Willy?" Dusty asked.

"I don't think so."

"How'd they talk?" Waco put in, beating Dusty to the question.

"It's hard to tell, the bandanas muffled their voices," Wallenheim replied. "I couldn't even say to their accents. But I don't think they were Texans."

At that moment the Kid appeared at the door with word that he could find no tracks. Dusty shrugged, having expected no more, and told the clerks that he would let them know if anything happened.

"Some of the cowhands're getting mite festive," the Kid remarked as they left the office. "We'd best circulate a bit and let 'em know we're around."

"Do you want me, Dusty?" Waco asked.

"No. You go see Babsy; Lon and me can handle things for once."

"Was I you, I'd change my pants first," the Kid continued.

Not until that moment did Waco remember the damp, muddy state of his clothing. However he hesitated before taking the Kid's advice.

"About that hold-up, Dusty—," the youngster began.

"Think about it for a spell," Dusty answered. "There's nothing much we can do until day-break anyways. Before you go to meet Babsy, write down a description of those two jaspers and tomorrow we'll see about running them down."

Much as Waco hated the thought of the delay, he knew it to be unavoidable. Not even the Kid could read sign in the dark and the law did not know in which direction to start the hunt. Anger at the two clerks rose again, but the youngster fought it down. In doing so, he started to think about what they had said. Before any conclusion took definite form, Waco found himself alone. Still thinking, he made his way back to the marshal's office, then to the hotel to carry out the Kid's suggestion.

12

All in the Line of Duty

"What's up, luv?" Babsy asked, interrupting her comments as she became aware that they fell on deaf ears.

"Huh?" Waco grunted.

"You've not heard a word I said," she told him indignantly.

On his return to the hotel, Waco had cleaned his gunbelt and Colts before thinking of changing clothes or taking a bath. When he reached the Fair Lady to collect Babsy, he found her in a considerable temper because the Buffalo's staff had struck back far quicker than expected. On hearing how the opposition were dressing, Buffalo Kate had made each of the girls remove several inches from her dress hem and reduce its neckline still further. All through the walk to the hotel, where they intended to eat supper before taking a stroll around town, Babsy heatedly discussed the situation.

"Sure I have," Waco lied. "You was telling me how the girls thought they ought to go to the Buffalo and snatch them bald-headed."

"Only I'd finished telling you that and was asking what the shooting we heard was all about."

"Somebody robbed the Schubert freight outfit."

"Oo! Did anybody get hurt?"

"Nope."

"How much did they lose?"

"Something over four thousand dollars."

"And they got away?" she asked, eyes wide with interest.

"Yeah," Waco agreed, then told her the full story.

Indignation flashed across Babsy's expressive face. "Oo! Just wait until I see that Gus Schubert. I'll tell him a thing or two."

"Forget it, honey," Waco said. "They weren't to know who I was."

"You could've been hurt—."

"I wasn't. So we'll leave it lie."

"Cap'n Fog don't know who did it, does he?" Babsy asked after a pause during which Waco sank once more into the reverie which she had noticed since starting the meal.

"No," Waco admitted.

"But you reckon you do," she said. "That's what's on your mind, isn't it?"

"You're a real smart lil gal, Babsy honey," Waco told her with a wry grin. "There's something sets wrong about that hold-up. I think—hell, I don't know what to think for sure. Only I know that whole game was played wrong."

"Look, luv," Babsy said gently, reaching over to take his hand. "Why don't we leave that look at the golden horseshoe nail until later? Miss Freddie'd like me to do some more singing tonight and you'll not settle easy until you've thought this lot out."

"If that's what you want."

"It's not. But you've got a face like a wet week and you'll not rest until you've done what you have to do."

"You're too smart for a pretty lil gal," Waco said, gently squeezing her hand. "I reckon I'd be mighty poor company tonight."

"I'd already thought that out," Babsy smiled.

On returning to the Fair Lady, Babsy went to change from her street clothes into something more suitable. Before leaving, Waco crossed to the bar and asked Vera a question to which she gave a negative answer. Outside he paused for a moment and then directed his feet towards the Buffalo. At that place's batwing doors he paused and looked piously into the sky.

"Babsy honey," he said. "This's all in the line of duty, as Mark'd say."

With that he entered and, despite tending to support the Fair Lady, had to admit that Buffalo Kate had come up with a right smart answer to Miss Freddie's challenge. Ginger came towards him, wearing a skirt cut so high that white flesh twinkled attractively over the black of her stockings.

"Hey there," she greeted. "Where's that fat foreigner who's usually hanging on to your shirt-tail?"

"I should be so lucky," Waco grinned. "Babsy told me to say 'howdy' for her—And afore you ask, I'm working."

"I never did have any luck," Ginger pouted and walked away.

Crossing to the counter, Waco leaned against it for a moment until Wally, the head bartender, noticed him. Since Waco's smooth handling of the two drunken buffalo-hunters, Wally had come to regard him as a real deputy, not merely a kid wearing a badge. So the bartender passed paying customers to greet the youngster.

"Boss says your money's no good here, Waco," he said. "What'll it be?"

"Just a beer," Waco replied and jerked his head towards the tables. "A man can sure work up a thirst just looking in here."

"Better'n at the Fair Lady, huh?"

"You don't reckon I'd be loco enough to admit that—or deny it," Waco grinned. "Say, Wally. Have any of the sod-buster kids been in spending more than usual tonight?"

In another town, questioned by the usual run of Kansas lawmen, Wally would have given deep thought before answering and chosen his words with care. Such was the respect Dusty's office had built up that the bartender did not hesitate to answer immediately.

"Naw. Couple of 'em come in earlier, bought a beer each and left."

"What'd they look like and how'd they dress?"

"One was about your size, the other shorter, they wore

108

jackets, pants, blue shirts and ties, I think. Didn't pay them much mind."

"The big one didn't wear a mackinaw, did he?" Waco asked.

"No. A store-bought jacket, they both did," Wally replied. "What's up?"

"Nothing much."

"You thinking about the hold-up at Schubert's?" asked the bartender. "Hell, neither of 'em was packing a gun—I noticed that much."

That figured, a man without a gun being something of a novelty. Waco did not offer to enlighten Wally as to the arms the robbers carried.

"Likely I'm wrong then," the youngster said, taking the glass of beer Wally poured. "Don't say anything about this. I don't want folks thinking I'm blaming the nesters."

"You can count on me," Wally assured him.

"Why sure I can," Waco grinned. "Especially as I saw you and Vera from the Fair Lady last night down to the livery barn."

"That was only busi—," Wally began. "No, damn it, if that's not worse'n what we was doing."

"Shame on you, sir," Waco chuckled. "Anyways, I won't talk if you don't."

A broad smile creased Wally's face. "An I thought Cap'n Fog had chased all the sharks out of town. If I see anything, I'll let you know."

"Send word to the office, I've got some more walking to do. Say, I'm getting to like walking—it's worrying the hell out of me."

With that the youngster finished his beer and set the glass on the counter. As he turned to leave, Wally spoke in an urgent voice:

"One thing, Waco. Vera and me—."

"Yep?"

"We don't talk about business—if you know what I mean."

"I reckon I do," Waco answered soberly. "And I never thought you did. See you, Wally."

"I'll be here," the bartender promised.

Leaving the Buffalo, Waco went next to the Wooden Spoon. There the entertainment emphasis lay on gambling rather than girls, so he regarded it as a less likely choice for the men he sought. On his arrival, Dongelon told him that no young nesters had been in all night and asked no questions about the query.

That seemed to close the matter, for the theatre and other saloons had yet to find owners. While there had been some inquiries about vacant businesses, the interested parties had lost their desire to purchase on learning of the town's gambling ordnance.

Deciding to pass his theories on to Dusty and learn what the small Texan thought of them, Waco walked towards the jail. As he approached the Buffalo Saloon, he saw something not entirely unusual taking place. Two brawny bouncers half-carried, half-dragged a struggling cowhand through the batwing doors and dumped him on the sidewalk.

"Those gals in here's for looking at, not touching up, young feller," one of the pair stated. "Happen you got them sort of ideas, go around to Lily Gouch's place and she'll fit you up good."

"Damn it!" Waco breathed. "What've I been using for brains? All that walking must've addled 'em."

Then he started forward at a faster pace as the cowhand sat up, reaching for a gun.

"Why you dirty Yankees, you!" yelled the cowhand. "I'll—."

"Shooting bouncers's plumb again the law, friend," Waco warned, blocking the other's draw with his foot. "And going to jail for trying it's nowheres near as much fun as going to Lily Gouch's place."

"I'd go there for sure, if I knew where the son-of-a-bitching place is," the cowhand replied, forcing himself erect.

"Come on then, I'll show you," Waco offered.

"Friend, you surely is a friend indeed," the cowhand replied, then peered closer at the badge on the youngster's vest. "Well I swan! You're a John Law."

"Yep. Showing you's all part of the town service."

"Whooee! Those jaspers from the OD Connected we met going home sure called it right when they said this was a square town. I've been hauled out of a house by a deputy more'n once. But this's the first time one ever took me there."

"I'm not sure I should be doing it myself," Waco answered with a grin.

For all that he escorted the cowhand through the town's back streets and pointed out Lily Gouch's house.

"You coming in?" asked the cowhand. "I'll stand treat."

"Now there's an offer I'm not likely to have beat," Waco smiled.

"Trouble being I can't take you up on it. The marshal don't approve of us deputies going on his time."

"He sounds's ornery as a trail boss."

"You can say that again. You go on in, friend and maybe one day I'll take you up on that offer."

"Feel free any ole time," grinned the cowhand and ambled up the garden path with some speed.

Waco stood watching until the cowhand had entered the building, then went towards the fence. Set in a clump of trees, so as to attract as little unwanted attention to itself as possible, the house was well-lit. So well that Waco could see the horses tied to the picket fence clearly enough to believe at least two did not belong to cowhands.

An obvious Indian pony stood at the end of the line, its Cheyenne-roll saddle bearing a fine-looking Sharps buffalo rifle in the boot. Most likely it belonged to a hide-hunter celebrating the end of a successful trip. After one glance Waco ignored the pony and moved along to more likely prospects.

Even had there only been the night's light to guide him, the youngster would have known two of the horses had never worked half-wild longhorn cattle. Bigger and heavier than range stock, they looked suitable for light-draught work, but too slow and clumsy to ride herd on. Nesters used such horses, capable of hauling wagon or plough, but able to be saddle-ridden when necessary.

Further proof of ownership came from studying the saddles on the big horses. First, each saddle had but a single girth. Lesser men might dally one end to the saddle when roping, so it could be hurriedly released in case of an emergency. Figuring to hang on to whatever he caught, the Texan knotted his rope to the horn. Doing so threw such a strain on the square-skirted Texas saddle that two girths—a son of the Lone Star State scorned to use the word 'cinch'—were needed to hold it in place. While smaller than the dinner-plate style fancied by Mexicans, each saddle's horn was larger than any Texan used.

Speaking gently to avoid disturbing the horses, Waco moved closer. His eyes went to the saddle boot of the nearer animal and he felt a thrill of excitement run through him as he saw it held a Ballard single-shot rifle. From there he looked at the coat fastened lining outwards to the cantle. Fanning open the folds, he exposed the outer surface and found it to be a red and black check. The other nester horse carried a black wolf-skin coat on its cantle, while a long, old twin-barrel, muzzle-loading shotgun hung in a primitive boot. Neither saddle toted the floursack used to take away the loot, which did not surprise the youngster.

After completing his study of the horses, Waco withdrew and paused to decide on his next course of action. A certain amount of antipathy always existed between farmers and cowhands, due to a clashing of interests. In Kansas a furrow ploughed around one's holdings rated as a fence under law, giving the owner the right to prosecute for trespass against anyone crossing it. Such 'furrow fences' were sometimes cut on each side of cattle trails, to keep the trail-herds within certain bounds; this was regarded by some outfits as an infringement of personal liberty. So far little actual hostility had developed between the two factions around Mulrooney. However the nesters might regard his suspicions as unwarranted, or even persecution of their kind if he arrested the horses' owners. True everything pointed to the pair being the men he wanted; but it could be no more than coincidence.

Check mackinaw jackets of every hue could be bought in most towns. Possessing long-lasting qualities, wolf-skins were much sought after to make coats. Few nesters, particularly in areas safe from Indian attack, spent money on modern weapons if they owned something capable of bringing down pot-meat or for occasional defence. Selling for from twenty-five to thirty dollars, as against the Winchester's thirty-eight to sixty, depending on quality and fittings, the Ballard single-shot rifle found much favour among nesters.

"Which means that there're plenty of mackinaws that colour, wolf-skin coats, Ballards 'n' old scatterguns around. Only not all together in one place—Or could there be?"

A more cautious young man would have headed back to the office and asked his experienced friends for advice. Yet while he did so, the two suspects might come from the house, collect their horses and head for home. If they left town and disposed of the identifiable clothing, there would be little chance of locating them or proving their part in the hold-up. Sure Waco could point out the horses if he saw them again, but he doubted if such evidence would go far in court.

Once again Waco decided to act on his own. If he should prove

112

wrong, his inexperience would offer Dusty an excuse when protesting friends of the accused came to call.

Opening the gate, Waco walked up to the house's front door and opened it. It was his first visit to Lily Gouch's establishment and he found that she had moved fast since her arrival. The main room, into which he stepped, had comfortable seats. Heavy curtains draped the windows, although they were left open so far. Seated at a piano, a Negro was playing a lively tune, while another coloured man stood behind a small combined bar and free-lunch counter. The few customers, all cowhands, and six or so girls looked curiously at the young deputy, but none offered to move in his direction. One of the girls darted to a side door, opened it and spoke to somebody on the other side.

Coming through the door, Lily Gouch showed some surprise at the sight of Waco. Then she crossed the room, a welcoming smile on her lips despite a wary glint in her eyes.

"Hey, deputy," she greeted. "Can I do something for you?"

"Yes, ma'am," he replied, then paused, not quite sure how to go on.

For a moment Lily's smile wavered and the suspicious gleam grew more intense. In other towns such a visit and comment usually heralded a request for some kind of funds, or the free services of one of the girls. So far there had ben no such demands made by either the peace officers or civic authorities in Mulrooney, but she could never shake off the uneasy feeling that it might start. So she waited to see how much, or for what reason, the bite would be put on her.

"You've got a couple of nester kids in here, ma'am," Waco said.

"Sure," Lily agreed and annoyance replaced the other emotions on her face. "Look, if their folks've been bitching about it, you tell them from me it's the first time they've been here and my gals didn't go out and drag 'em in with ropes."

"I don't reckon their folks know they're here, ma'am," Waco assured her, pleased that his theories had proved correct so far. "There's no need to get riled."

"Damn it, deputy, being treated fair's spoiling me," Lily said with a grin. "I was never this touchy when I had to hand over 'campaign funds' or pay up every time anybody felt they'd a grief against me. Have a drink?"

"A cup of Arbuckle's'd go down good, ma'am."

"Anything else? Lily inquired, darting a glance around the room.

"No offence, ma'am," Waco replied, "but all I want's to talk about them two nester kids. How long've they been in?"

"Look. I don't like talking about my visitors where anybody can see me. It's not good for business. Come into the office and have that cup of coffee while we talk."

Although not as plushly furnished as the main room, Lily's office offered a fair amount of comfort. Taking the comfortable chair she pointed out, Waco sank into it with a grin.

"You should try the chairs in our office," he told her. "Would you mind if we left the door open, so's I can see if those nesters come in?"

"Nobody'll tell them you're here—."

"You're getting touchy again, ma'am."

"Damned if I'm not! Sure, I'll open the door for you."

When sure he could see into the main room, Waco settled back in the chair and continued the questioning.

"When'd you say they came in, ma'am?"

"Maybe half an hour or so back. They're upstairs with two of the gals now."

"For the night?"

"At my prices?" Lily scoffed. "I was surprised to see 'em come in for a short time even."

"They didn't have much money then?" Waco asked, feeling a mixture of relief and disappointment.

"Do their kind ever?" Lily sniffed. "Their folks make eating-money at most and not much of that. Like I said, I was surprised to see 'em come in here. And I'll bet this's the first time they've been into a house, or paid for it."

"They shouldn't be long afore they're coming down then?"

"Not with a dollar 'short time'."

"Mind if I stay on in here and look them over when they do?"

A madam, even in a town like Mulrooney, could not easily refuse any request made by a peace officer. In addition to knowing that, Lily felt she owed the marshal's office consideration for their treatment since her arrival. While not sure just what Waco's interest in the two young nesters might be, she decided to help him all she could.

"Stay as long as you like,' she said. "I'll have some food sent in. Say, what've they done?"

114

"I don't know as they've done anything," Waco admitted. "That's what I want to find out."

"Huh huh. Do me a favour, will you?"

"If I can."

"Don't jump them in here. I wouldn't want the marks getting the idea I'd sic the law on 'em."

"I'll not make a move until they leave," Waco promised. "Is there another way out of here?"

"Through that door over there," Lily replied. "I'll keep 'em talking for long enough to let you get through the garden and over the fence."

"That'd do fine, ma'am," the youngster said.

Lily shook her head as she walked out of the office and left the door open enough for her guest to watch the room. Never had she met such an accommodating lawman. Most peace officers, even honest ones, would not have been so considerate even though she co-operated with them.

"Damned if I've ever been in such a town afore," she told herself in a mystified voice and went to order a meal for Waco.

13

Lord, What a Fool Mistake

Sitting in Lily Gouch's office, nursing a plate loaded with slices of ham, chicken and other choice items selected from the free-lunch counter, Waco again gave thought to his conclusions about the hold-up. He went through each item in its turn, examining it as he ate and watched the main room. All he knew increased the belief that he had called the play right.

No matter that the clerks at the freight office thought they were victims of the James brothers, or at least of Tricky Dick Cansole's gang, Waco felt certain that greenhorns had pulled the robbery.

Take the weapons the thieves used for a starter. While a double-barrelled ten-gauge shotgun might be unequalled as a pacifier, it could not be termed an ideal weapon for an outlaw. Nor did a single-shot rifle strike Waco as the kind of weapon an experienced owlhoot would carry. Neither the rifle nor the shotgun offered ease of concealment and both lacked the potential for sustained rapid fire in case of a fight.

Although successful and profitable, the hold-up had been carried out in a most amateurish manner. On entering the office, the thieves had taken the clerks' wallets and watches before going to the money-loaded safe. More than that, they had failed to bring along a container capable of toting off a large sum of money and had to use a floursack that chanced to be in the room. Men who knew their business would never have left the clerks free, even if face down on the floor, to endanger their escape. Nor would they have left the lamp illuminating the outside stairs lit while they went down, allowing themselves to be clearly seen by anyone passing by.

No, nothing in the way the two robbers had acted led him to believe they were experienced outlaws.

Before Waco had half finished his snack, he saw two young men coming down the stairs. Even without Lily going towards them, he would have known them to be the pair he wanted. Dressed in cheap, poorly-fitting town suits, they looked like any other young nesters in town for a celebration. They fitted the scanty descriptions of the robbers, although Waco could not state positively that he recognised them.

Thinking back, Waco remembered seeing the two young men in the Fair Lady and recalled their behavior when losing the girls to the more prosperous cowhands. Neither wore a revolver and he could see nothing to hint they carry a concealed weapon of any kind. One thing was for sure. The two nesters did not look or act like owlhoots.

"If I'm wrong—," Waco mused, rising and putting his plate on Lily's desk. "Damn it, a whole lot points to them. I'll take a chance."

With that he crossed to the rear door and let himself out of the building. Crossing the garden, he vaulted the picket fence and moved around to where the nesters' horses stood. From what he had seen, the taller of the pair looked the kind to take rash chances. So the youngster decided to nullify the risk. Quickly he slid the Ballard partly from its boot. Always eager to learn, he had taken the opportunity offered by being a deputy to study the various weapons on sale in town. Among them were several Ballard rifles, a popular item among folks who did not wish to pay a high price yet wanted a reliable weapon. So he knew how to operate the rifle's mechanism. Thrusting down the trigger guard opened the breech, but he had to work the sliding stud under the frame to extract the bullet. With the rifle rendered harmless, he replaced it and went to the shotgun. Disarming this proved easier, for all he needed to do was remove the percussion caps from the nipples and he did not even have to draw it from the boot to do so.

Light glowed as the front door opened. Waco drew back from the horses and crouched down, watching the nesters come along the path to the front gate. Laughing, shoving each other, they looked to be in excellent spirits.

"That was good, Vic," the smaller of the pair announced. "Say, that gal I went with told me she was a Russian countess—What's that?"

"A pack of lies, I'd say," Vic answered in a tone of worldly wisdom.

"We'll have to go in there again. For the whole night next time."

"Maybe, Tommy. Maybe."

"Aw, Vic. We can afford to now."

"Sure but we don't want folks noticing that, do we?" Vic replied, walking to his horse's head.

"Hold it right there!" Waco ordered, drawing and cocking his right hand Colt as he moved forward.

"Wha—!" Tommy began, spinning around.

"Do what he says, Tommy," Vic said, just a shade too calmly. "If you're looking to rob us, mister, you'll have mighty slim pickings."

With that he lunged forward, scooped the Ballard from the boot, lined it waist high in Waco's direction then squeezed the trigger. Only a dull, dry click rewarded his efforts and a startled curse broke from him.

"The scatter's got no caps on it either," Waco warned as Vic dropped the Ballard and swung towards Tommy's horse. "And I'm a deputy marshal, not an owlhoot."

Give Vic his due, he knew enough to yell 'calf-rope' and quit. Instead of trying to get around Tommy's mount to the useless shotgun, he stood fast.

"What's up, deputy?" Tommy asked in a worried voice.

"Let's take a walk down to the jail house and talk about it, shall we?" Waco replied.

"Why'd you want us?" Tommy began. "We don't know any—."

"Hush up, Tommy boy!" Vic interrupted, speaking in a mixture of urgent warning and reassurance. "Likely the deputy reckons he knows what he's doing. Just for the hell of it, though, what's up, deputy?"

"I figured you'd know that," Waco told him. "Let's go."

"Anything you say, you're pointing the gun. How about our hosses?"

"Take them along—from the right side."

Most white men mounted their horses from the left, so the animals became accustomed to it and showed a marked reluctance to letting a rider go up on the right side. Waco doubted if the nesters had taken the time to train their mounts in accepting them coming up to the saddle from the 'Indian side', so ordered them to lead from the right to lessen their chances of escape.

As he walked along behind the pair, placed so that he could observe them both and counter any hostile moves, Waco studied them. Watching and listening, he noticed that Vic did most of the talking. It almost seemed that the taller nester set out to jolly his companion on, or relieve the other's anxiety. At first the attempt met with no success. Tommy still continued to act nervous and scared.

"Ole Tommy's worried about what his pappy'll say," Vic remarked over his shoulder to Waco. "Him being arrested after just coming out of a goosing-ranch and all."

"Yeah," Tommy went on with the air of one suddenly presented with the answer to a problem. "Paw's not going to like it."

"Let's hope he doesn't have anything worse not to like," Waco answered dryly. "Only we all know he will."

"Hell, you can't arrest us for going into Lily's place," Vic replied. "At least I've never heard about it if you can. And the jails'd be full if you start."

Waco ignored the comment, but noticed that some of Tommy's nervousness appeared to be going. Possibly the smaller nester's worry did rise from the cause Vic suggested. Kansas dirt-farmers had a reputation among cowhands for being pious, church-going folk strong against all kinds of sin. So Tommy might feel concern, if not fear, at his father's reaction to learning where he

118

had spent the evening.

Although the youngster could form no opinion as to the likeliness of their guilt or innocence, he felt sure that he had guessed correctly. Most likely Dusty knew of a way to reach the truth. It would be interesting to see how the small Texan handled the affair.

Once again Waco started to show his instinctive flair for law enforcement. He decided against taking his prisoners in through the front of the building. Doing so meant going along the main street, in full view of anybody who chanced to be on it. Possibly other nesters were in town and he wanted to keep the pair's arrest a secret until after Dusty had interviewed them. So he directed them to go to the rear of the building and leave their horses at the small civic pound corral.

As Waco escorted his prisoners towards the pole-walled pound, he saw a human shape drawing away from the rear of the office building. Having retained his Colt in hand while bringing in the two nesters, he did not need to draw it and tensed ready to meet any trouble that might start. It seemed highly unlikely that any other dirt-farmers knew of the pair's fate, or would try to take them from his custody by force, but he still watched the approaching shape. Drawing closer though it might be, he still could not say for sure whether it be man or woman. Whoever it was could have come through the alley from the street, or been at the rear of the building.

If it should be the latter, there might be some fuss. Waco knew the position of Smith's cell and remembered Dusty's comments about the Cansole gang attempting to contact the captured outlaw. Should that figure be one of the gang, he might take exception to coming up against a deputy.

Then Waco realised that the approaching shape was a woman dressed in flowing clothes of a special kind. As she came closer, he recognised her as the new mother-superior from the convent. She slackened her pace on seeing the three young men, darting a glance around her.

"Howdy ma'am," Waco greeted. "I sure hope we didn't spook you too much."

"Oh! It's you, deputy," she answered, walking forward. "Good evening. I've been asked to come out and see one of our people who's taken sick."

"Can you find the place, ma'am?"

"Yes. I've been to see her before."

With that the woman passed by and Waco continued to head his prisoners in the direction of the pound. After fastening their horses to the central horizontal pole, the two young men went to the rear door. Watching them all the time, Waco reached around and knocked on it.

"Yeah?" came Pickle-Barrel's voice.

"Southrons hear your country call you," Waco replied, using the first line of General Samuel Pike's words to the tune 'Dixie'. During the War, the same line served as a password between Confederate spies.

When making plans to circumvent other escape efforts, Dusty had decided on the words as a sign to let the jailer know a friend requested admittance. So Pickle-Barrel did not hesitate to open the door. That he held his old Colt Dragoon showed no lack of faith, only a commendable sense of caution.

"Who're this pair?" the old-timer inquired, eyeing the nesters up and down.

"Couple of gents I reckon Dusty'll want to meet," Waco replied.

"Best make 'em welcome then," Pickle-Barrel declared, waving the nesters inside and re-locking the door after Waco had entered. "You gents don't mind if we'ns go through with the formalities, I reckon."

"You seem to know what it's all about," Vic answered calmly. "I'm damned if I do, but I'll go along with you."

"Thankee," grunted the old jailer, darting a long glance at Vic's face. Then he swung his attention to Waco. "You searched 'em yet?"

"Figured to wait until I could see what I was doing first," the youngster replied. "It's allus as well. Only let's do it in the back here."

"It's your game, young feller," Pickle-Barrel stated, although he could guess why Waco had made the request. "You watch the lil 'un while I tend to his pard."

Keeping guard while the jailer deftly searched first Vic, then Tommy, Waco felt a growing concern. The contents of their pockets proved to be nothing more nor less than one might expect; a jack-knife, some string, handkerchieves, not more than five dollars between them and a battered old watch which certainly did not belong to either of the robbed clerks.

Towards the end of the very thorough search, Dusty and the Kid walked into the office. They came through to the rear at Waco's call and listened to his reasons for bringing in the pair of nesters. However Dusty's reaction when told came as a complete surprise to Waco.

"You reckon *this* pair could've pulled the hold-up?" Dusty demanded in a disbelieving tone after studying the pitiful contents of their pockets.

"Sure I do!" the youngster answered.

"Lordy lord! Did you-all hear that, Lon?"

"I heard it, but I can't hardly believe it," the Kid replied. "Lord. What a fool mistake."

Annoyance and shock played on Waco's face at his friends' outspoken condemnation. Even if he had made a bad mistake, he did not expect such an open display of criticism. Malicious grins came to Vic and Tommy's faces, while they started to look more confident.

"I thought you'd learned better, boy," Dusty stated and Waco writhed at the use of a name normally only applied in private. "Damn it, that hold-up was pulled by two *men*, not by a couple of milk-cow churn-twisters."

"I told you we hadn't done nothing!" Tommy scoffed, but his lips remained in the tight line they had formed when Dusty used the cowhand's derogatory name for nesters. At his side, Vic stirred restlessly and scowled at the small Texan.

"And he told you right," Dusty went on, derision plain in voice and expression. "Whoever robbed the freight outfit had brains and guts."

"This pair of two-buckle boys couldn't find their mouths with a fork-load of food 'cept on a bright summer afternoon," the Kid went on. "Here's us been out hunting fellers slick enough to have pulled that stick-up and you waste time hauling in fool-hoemen."

Fury flickered on Vic's face at the words. "Hey!—." he began.

"Damn it, throw them out of here!" Dusty barked. "I haven't time to waste on sod-busters when I'm looking for the *men* who robbed that place."

"You've found 'em!" Tommy yelled, furious at the scornful dismissal.

"Shut it!" Vic shouted.

"Go on, get them the hell out of here!" Dusty snapped. "I—."

"I tell you we did rob the freight outfit!" Tommy insisted, wild with anger at the continued contemptuous rejection.

"Then where's the money?" Dusty barked.

"We hid it outs—."

"You stupid son-of-a-bitch!" Vic howled. "You've fixed our wagon now."

With that he flung himself through the door into the office and returned even faster, propelled by a thrust of Mark Counter's good arm. Knowing his presence would not be needed in the rear of the building, Mark had remained in the front and was in an ideal position to prevent the nester's attempt at escape. Fury showed on Vic's face as he returned. Screeching curses, he flung himself at his friend, laid hold of Tommy's lapels and slammed him against the wall. The Kid and Waco moved forward fast, catching Vic's arms and hauling him away from the scared Tommy. Even then the raging nester continued to struggle, but could not escape from their hold.

"Toss him in the cells," Dusty ordered and turned to Tommy. "I reckon you'd best tell me all about it."

Watching Pickle-Barrel spring to and open the door of a cell, then the two deputies thrust Vic inside, gave Tommy a chance to realise what his incautious words meant. Like most nester youths, Tommy resented the more affluent cowhands. Seeing them at the end of a drive, relaxed, with plenty of money to spend, he overlooked the way they earned their pay. Forgetting, or not knowing of the long hours worked, risks taken, dangers endured, while bringing the cattle north, he saw only men his own age who appeared to have advantages that never came his way.

It had long been Tommy's view that, given the same chance, he could lick anything done by a cowhand. So the thought that such an insignificant specimen of the cow-chasing breed regarded him with contempt spurred him to folly. The fact that none of the three Texans greatly exceeded him in age, with the tall blond kid even younger, drove all Vic's warning from his mind. So he blurted out that damning admission. Yet, having been granted time to think, he decided to bluff things out.

"I don't know what you mean," he said, swinging to face Dusty.

"Shucks, we've known all along you did it," the small Texan replied breezily. "All you did was tell us what we knew."

"So prove it."

Ever since they fled from the freight outfit's office, Vic had been telling Tommy that nothing could be proved against them. The older youngster's insistence originally filled his friend with confidence. While it had been badly shaken, the feeling returned as Tommy realised one vital piece of evidence was missing.

"That'll be easy enough," Dusty answered calmly. "The deputy who brought you in recognised you straight off—and the two clerks'll know your faces."

If Dusty hoped for a denial on the grounds that Vic and Tommy were wearing masks, the nester never gave it. Just in time Tommy bit down on the words as they rose to boil out in triumph.

"Maybe he figures the one they shot can't talk, Dusty," the Kid remarked.

"Sh—Shot?" Tommy gasped.

"We heard the shooting, that's what got us there so quick," Dusty told him. "And we'd've been after you a whole heap faster happen there hadn't been the shot clerk to tend to."

Standing back against the wall, where he had retired in the face of his two friends' attitude, Waco watched everything. Slowly the opinion formed that he had missed something. Yet he could not be sure what. So he followed some advice Dusty once gave him on the matter of what to do when unsure of the next move; he did nothing.

"Look, we never shot nobody!" Tommy gasped, looking from Dusty to the Kid.

"That's what they all say," Pickle-Barrel commented. "One feller told us we couldn't prove it 'cause nobody saw the bullet leave the gun."

"He'd a right smart legal point," drawled the Kid. "What'd you do?"

"Hung him for something we knowed he'd done."

"H—Hung—!" gulped Tommy, hands going almost automatically to his neck. "Y—You can't—."

"Not unless the feller dies," Dusty admitted. "Waco, go ask Mark if any word's come in yet."

"I tell you we never shot off our guns!" Tommy yelled. "Sure we robbed the freight office, but we didn't shoot anybody."

"Let's go into the office and hear what you've got to tell," Dusty said.

Seated before the marshal's desk, with the deputies forming a half-circle around him and Dusty on the other side holding pen to paper, Tommy hesitantly told his story. Coming to town, short of money as usual, the two young nesters had grown discontented at the sight of numerous pleasures beyond their slender purse. Everybody else seemed to have plenty to spend and they felt the deficit badly. A foolish attempt to increase their finances at a faro table ended in disaster and wiped out the little cash they owned.

One of the rules Freddie had brought in when she opened her place was 'broke-money'. Anybody who reached the blanket either drinking or trying to lick the house's percentage on the gambling games, could apply to one of the barmaids and receive five dollars. While collecting their 'broke-money', the nesters had overheard the freight outfit's swamper cursing the clerks for sending him to fetch a bucket of beer while they worked on the accounts.

Urging Tommy to leave, Vic put up the proposal that they should rob the clerks. Although Tommy had raised several objections, Vic produced answers for them all. Wearing the mackinaw and wolf-skin coat to hide their suits, and masked by their bandanas, they could not be recognised. Nor would Schubert and Wallenheim argue in the face of the shotgun. Robbing them would be too easy.

Raised to the point of bravado by the beer he had drunk before losing the rest of his money at faro, and smarting under the failure to attract a saloongirl, Tommy went along with the scheme. Neither expected such a windfall as came their way via the open safe, their first idea being merely to take the clerks' wallets; although Vic decided to take the watches and give the affair a professional flavour. Finding the safe open, they had made the most of the chance.

Although they had never heard of Tricky Dick Cansole's methods—Dusty kept the story of the stashed loot known only to his deputies—the nesters had hit on the same idea. Taking only enough money for a visit to Lily Gouch's house, they hid the rest outside town.

"I'll show you where," Tommy promised, looking and sounding close to tears as understanding of his position grew stronger on him.

"Go with him, Waco, Lon," Dusty ordered.

A somewhat indignant Waco accompanied the Kid to collect their horses. For a time he expected the Kid to make some comment, but none came. Unable to hold down his feelings any longer, the youngster let out an explosive snort.

"Damn it all, Lon!" he said hotly. "I sure never expected Dusty to roust me out like that. Especially when it comes out that I'm right."

Instead of giving any condolences, the Kid broke into a deep, hearty chuckle and slapped his companion on the back.

"Don't that beat all," the Kid finally got out.

"What's so funny, 'cepting you near on bust my back-bone?" Waco howled indignantly.

"For somebody who's acted real smart up 'til now, you're sure showing poor sense," the Kid replied.

"Huh?"

"You handled everything just right, boy. All the way."

Realisation struck the youngster, slamming him to a halt. Catching hold of the Kid's arm, Waco swung him around and thrust a wrathful face up close to the other's Indian-dark, grinning features.

"You mean that you'n' Dusty figured all along I'd got the right fellers?"

"I'd have to say 'yes' to that," the Kid admitted. "See, me 'n' ole Dusty maybe don't have half the gals in town running themselves ragged chasing us, but we can count to ten if we go slow and use all our fingers. We reckoned that hold-up hadn't been pulled by regular outlaws and's soon's things quietened down a mite we started asking questions. Then what do we find?"

"Try telling me."

"We find that our 'good-looking, young one's' already been 'round asking the same questions, only sooner."

"You couldn't miss guessing who they meant when they said 'the good-looking young one'," Waco said in a milder tone.

"Took us a while, but we figured it out," the Kid replied. "Anyways, we got to Lily Gouch's place in time to see you coming out stuffed to the craw with turkey and ham and all them other things *we*'d've had if you hadn't been so blasted nosy. Figured that seeing's you'd had the goodies, you might's well do the work and sat back to let you. You handled it good, boy. Real good."

"So why'd you and Dusty start raw-hiding me?" Waco demanded, noting that the word 'boy' took on its old connotation; implying that he might be young, but he would grow from a boy into a real good man.

"Do I need to tell you?"

"Naw. He figured to rile them nesters into speaking up like lil Georgie Washingtons. 'I can't tell a lie, I chopped down that slippery elm' or something."

"Way I heard it, it was a chestnut tree he chopped down," grinned the Kid. "Anyways, there wasn't a son-of-a-bitching thing to prove they were the pair that snuck off with Pop Schubert's hard-earned wealth—We stood outside listening—So Dusty reckoned they might fall for an old trick—."

"Making out that you didn't reckon nesters, especially them two, was smart or brave enough to do it."

"Sure. Like I said. It's an old trick, but it still works when you pull it on wet-behind-the-ears buttons—on both sides of the fence."

"Yah!" Waco jeered. "I knowed all along what the game was, and that it'd work right."

"You should've told me which way it'd go then."

"Why?"

"I was betting that Vic jasper'd break first—unless you did."

"Gambling'll be your ruin for certain sure," Waco grinned. "Come on, stop holding me back. I want to wind up *my* arrest and go see Babsy."

"Yes sir, deputy," the Kid replied. "And you've sure earned it."

Escorted by the two Texans, Tommy rode from town and led the way to the hiding place of the loot. From the hollow trunk of an old oak tree the young nester drew the floursack and two hats. Using the same half-smart thinking that had led them to hide the proceeds of their robbery, the pair had also left the hats which might identify them. Then, like all beginners, they made a mistake by failing to dispose of their coats and weapons.

With the loot returned to the office and his prisoners bedded down for the night, Waco declared that he had done enough for one watch. Displaying an air of condescension his friends felt he deserved, the younster announced that such menial tasks as gathering up the crop of drunks was beneath his dignity. However he made sure that he stood at the open front door when he said it and departed before reprisals could be uttered against his person.

Going to the Fair Lady, he attracted Babsy's attention and quickly resumed the state of affairs that handling his first crime had caused to be interrupted. Later that night, with Babsy snuggled up to him, Waco went to sleep conscious of having done a real good job of work.

14

I Figure I owe Him that Much

"Waal, Smithy boy, ole Tricky Dick's not got 'round to hauling you out of here yet," Pickle-Barrel remarked cheerfully as he carried a food tray into the solo cell at noon on Friday.

Standing with his back to the far wall of the cell, Smith darted a glance past the old jailer. As always one of the deputies stood in the passage ready to back Pickle-Barrel up in case of trouble. Trying to escape under those conditions seemed almost certain to end in failure.

"There's time," Smith answered with a casual shrug. "If I knew Tricky Dick and needed him to get me out, that is."

"You'll have me believing it soon," Pickle-Barrel said dryly. "Now me, I'd say he'd found that money and don't give a whoop in hell what we do with you."

"Maybe one day you'll get somebody to tell me what you're yapping about," Smith replied. "Can I come get my chow now, or do you figure I'd be loco enough to jump you and get shot trying to escape?"

"It'd be quicker than waiting for Tricky Dick to come pry you loose," the old timer commented and backed out of the cell.

Despite figuring that Smith would wait for Cansole to rescue him, Dusty had ordered that no chances must be taken. At no time would Pickle-Barrel open the cell door, unless a deputy stood on hand to cover him and even then Smith must be made to back as far away as the cell walls allowed before the jailer entered. As a further precaution nobody went into the cell wearing a gun, but left all weapons with the man in the passage.

The comments on Tricky Dick's failure to effect a rescue were not made out of spite, or to goad Smith into a foolish attempt to escape, but with the intention of lessening his faith in his boss. After the first unsuccessful try Smith began to show signs of concern, which increased a little with each passing day. Yet there appeared to be a complete change in his attitude, as Pickle-Barrel remarked upon while leaving the cell.

"He's still not giving anything away," Waco commented.

"Nope. He was getting a leedle mite worried, but he's perked up considerable again," Pickle-Barrel answered, closing and locking the door.

"Here, take this fool cannon back," Waco ordered, holding out the jailer's highly-prized Dragoon Colt by gripping the top of its barrel between the tips of thumb and forefinger. "I thought only a danged Injun'd be mean enough to tote a rusted-up relic like this."

"Injuns is smart on some things," Pickle-Barrel replied as they walked towards the front office.

"What's up with us Injuns now?" demanded the Kid, seated at the desk and having heard enough to be alert for an attack on himself.

"You got two-three hours to spare?" Waco wanted to know.

"We was just talking about my handgun," Pickle-Barrel went on!

Being a stout advocate of Colt's thum-busting four pound, nine ounce predecessor to the streamlined, light-weight—comparatively speaking—1860 Army Model revolver, the Kid often found himself called upon to defend its virtues against attacks by supporters of the later gun.

"It's the only thing you showed any sense in since I've knowed you," he told the jailer.

"How's Smith this morning?" Dusty asked before the wrangling could start.

"Right chirpy, Cap'n," Pickle-Barrel replied.

Before any more could be said, a small, dirty, sly-looking man wearing worn range clothes entered the office. While he dressed cowhand style, he did not have the appearance of one who worked the long hours needed to handle cattle.

"Is the marshal here?" he asked, darting nervous glances around him.

128

"That's me," Dusty replied. "What can I do for you?"

"I'd like to speak to you—in private like."

Taking in the man's nervous attitude, Dusty guessed what kind of mission brought him to the office. The small Texan knew also that the visitor would not talk in the presence of witnesses.

"Don't you bunch have work to do?" he growled, looking at the deputies.

"Why sure," agreed the Kid. "Let's go around town and see what's doing, boy."

"I'll teach you how to catch owlhoots while we're out," Waco promised, heading for the door.

"Time I looked in on the other prisoners," Pickle-Barrel continued. "Mind if I shut the door behind me, Cap'n?"

"Not this time," Dusty answered.

Left alone with Dusty, the man darted another worried look around, with particular emphasis on the street outside the windows. Then he turned to face the small Texan and said, "I got something mighty important to tell you, marshal."

"What?"

"It's been a long, hard ride here and I'm losing money all the time I'm away from my spread—."

"So?"

"What I've got's worth something."

"Try telling me and *I'll* be the judge of that."

"How much is it worth?" demanded the man, studying Dusty's insignificant, young appearance and making a mistake.

"Try me first," Dusty countered.

"But—!" the man began.

"I'm busy, *hombre*," Dusty growled, pushing back his chair. "You've got until I reach the door and put my hat on to let me know what's brought you here."

"There's a bunch of Texas owlhoots in town!" the man said hurriedly.

Sitting down again, Dusty took out his wallet and extracted a five dollar bill. "Here," he said, dropping it on the desk.

"Is that all?" the man squawked, reaching for the money.

"You've not told me anything worth even that much yet," Dusty snapped, catching the scrawny hand before it closed on the five dollar bill.

Surprise and pain twisted the man's face at the unexpected

strength with which Dusty gripped him. At that moment he stopped regarding the grim-faced Texan as insignificant, young or small and realised that he faced a big, tough, experienced peace officer with whom it would not pay to trifle.

"They're at Lily Gouch's place right now, waiting to meet up with one of Tricky Dick Cansole's boys," he yelped.

"You're sure?" Dusty demanded, thrusting the other's hand from him.

"I'd swear to it on a stack of Bibles shoulder high," the man replied.

"Now that *would* convince me," Dusty assured him dryly. "Who is it down there, Dick Dublin, Alf Marlow, Bill Brooken—."

"It's Smokey Hill Thompson and three of his boys," the man interrupted.

Only with an effort did Dusty prevent his surprise showing. Looking at his cold, grim face, the man never realised just how big a shock he had handed the small Texan. When Dusty did not speak, the man decided to strengthen his case.

"They're wanted down in Texas—."

"But there's no warrant out for them here in Kansas," Dusty pointed out. "If you figure on using me to collect a reward, mister, you've come to the wrong man."

"I'm only doing my right 'n' civic duty," the man said sullenly. "Ain't you going to do nothing about it?"

"Sure. I'm going to see H—Thompson, if it's him, and tell him to ride out of Edwards County. Thanking you right kindly for doing your civic duty, of course."

"Five dollars ain't a whole heap for the time I've lost," whined the man.

"It's plenty for something I don't know's true or not," Dusty pointed out. "After I get back from Lily's, I'll see if it's worth more."

"Aw, the five'll do," the man sighed. "I'll take it and be on my w—."

"Pickles!" Dusty called and the jailer ambled in.

"Yeah, Cap'n?"

"Keep this jasper entertained until I come back—and see he stays here until then."

"I'll do just that," promised the old timer, waving the man into a chair. "Set, friend. I sure hopes you like a good game of

130

cribbage, ain't none of the fellers in the cells can play a lick."

As he left the office, Dusty saw Mark coming along the street. Aware that the man's information might be a trick to clear the building for another escape bid, Dusty halted and told the blond giant to keep guard until he returned.

"Let me fetch Frank along to do that, Dusty," Mark suggested after hearing what news the man brought. "Then I'll go with you."

"I'm going alone, Mark," Dusty replied. "If we both go, there might be trouble."

"And there'll be two of us to handle it," Mark answered. "You know Hill's had some hard cusses riding with him."

"Sure. And I know we've been good friends for a lot of years. I figure I owe him that much, Mark."

"If you're set on it—."

"Real set. If Hill's only here for a meeting, there'll be no fuss. And if it's a smart move to clear the jail, I'd as soon not fall for it."

"Likely you'll be right," Mark said with a faint grin. "Like always. Only Dusty—."

"Yeah?"

"Don't get your hands too far from your guns."

Concern gnawed at Mark as he watched Dusty walk away. While Smokey Hill Thompson used to be a cheerful, amiable jasper and a spirited companion on a spree in town, life as a wanted outlaw might have changed him. Yet Mark knew why Dusty insisted on going alone to the meeting.

Turning, Mark collided with Big Sarah as she and Derringer approached the office door.

"Hey—!" the female deputy began.

"Sarah, you're lovely," Mark told her, gripping her shoulders and planting a kiss on her hung-open mouth. "And so're you, Frank. Stay put in the office until we get back."

Before either of the amazed pair could ask questions, Mark strode off along the street at a fast pace. Blushing just a mite, Sarah scratched her head and turned a baffled face to the grinning, if puzzled, gambler.

"What in hell—?" she began.

"Damned if I know, Sarah," Derringer admitted frankly. "I'll never understand cowhands."

Not knowing that Dusty had gone alone to face four outlaws,

131

Waco and the Kid strolled leasurely through the better section of town. Their route took them by the convent and they studied it with the curiosity most men feel at the sight of women who voluntarily cut themselves off from the normal pleasures of life.

"They're not doing much work outside today," Waco commented, seeing only three nuns in the grounds.

"Maybe the new mother superior wants the inside fixed first," the Kid replied. "She's some looker, for a nun."

"She's a looker for any kind of gal," Waco corrected, seeing the woman in question stood by the front door, then came walking across the garden as they drew nearer.

The same novice was still working at painting the fence. On hearing the deputies drawing nearer, she looked around. For a moment she seemed to be on the verge of speaking, but the mother superior reached her side.

"Good afternoon, gentlemen," the beautiful woman greeted. "There's nothing wrong, I hope."

"No, ma'am. Just making the rounds," the Kid replied.

"Go to the house, Sister Teresa," the woman ordered and, after a moment's hesitation, the novice obeyed. Then the woman looked at the deputies. "I must ask you not to come around here any more than is absolutely necessary."

"How's that, ma'am?" asked the Kid.

"You must understand that our order places a great strain upon us. Living under a vow of silence is far from easy for a woman, without further diversions."

"I reckon it must be, ma'am," the Kid agreed.

"It is especially hard upon a novice such as Sister Teresa," the mother superior went on. "Seeing two good-looking young men like yourself adds greatly to the strain. I'm sure neither of you wish to make her task any harder."

"No, ma'am," Waco said.

"I haven't seen Sister Bridget around since you came, ma'am," the Kid remarked, watching the novice enter the building.

For a moment some emotion flickered across the mother superior's face, coming and going too fast for the Texans to identify it. Then she replied, "With my arrival Sister Bridget is once more under the vow of silence. It is such a trial that she is segregating herself until learning to accept it again. You won't forget what I asked, will you?"

"No, ma'am," the Kid replied and, seeing that the woman clearly wanted to bring the meeting to an end, went on. "Let's get going, Waco."

"Sure," the youngster replied. "We'll bear what you said in mind, ma'am."

With that the deputies turned and walked away. The mother superior stood watching them go for a time and then returned to the door of the convent but did not enter. Instead she remained outside, watching the remaining nuns work.

15

I'll Stop You if I Have To

Walking towards the brothel's front door, Dusty thought out the variety of tasks a lawman faced during his day's work. That morning he had seen the fathers of the two nesters and, after some patient argument, convinced them that their sons came to be under arrest for committing a crime, not out of cowhand-farmer spite. Then he arranged with the judge for the pair to be let out on bail until their trial, and saw the current gathering over over-night offenders fined and released. After that he had hoped to be able to call Freddie Woods and Cattle Kate together to request an end to the way the feud developed, but the informer arrived before he could do so. Now he went to face an old friend turned outlaw, meaning to make the other leave Mulrooney and Edwards County before attempting a robbery.

Silence dropped on the room as Dusty walked in. Only four girls were present, gathered around the table seating the house's four customers. Dressed in cowhand clothes that showed signs of hard travelling, not even the low hanging guns set the quartet apart in appearance from a freshly-arrived trail crew. Two were of middle-age, tough, durable, experienced long-riders with alert watchful ways. The third, more of a dandy than his companions, had fewer years behind him and showed a raw brashness that spelled trouble to Dusty's knowing eyes.

However Dusty's main attention went to the man he remembered as a very brave, capable cavalry officer and competent rancher. In some way Smokey Hill Thompson did not appear changed from their last meeting. Tall, tanned, good looking in a rugged way, dressed as neatly as possible under the conditions, that was the same. Yet his face carried hard lines, the mouth no longer grin-quirked and merry, an alert wolf-caution replacing the humour.

If the girls did not know their guests' identity, they guessed at the nature of the men's employment. While Dusty crossed the floor, Lily's employees withdrew from the table. All three of Thompson's companions studied Dusty, but the older pair clearly waited for instructions.

"Howdy, Hill," Dusty greeted, halting at the table's edge across from his one-time friend.

"You wanting something with us, badge?" demanded the youngest of the four.

"Afore you start something that you can't finish, Joey," Thompson put in. "This here's Dusty Fog and he's my *amigo*. Howdy, Dusty. I haven't seen you in a coon's age."

"I tried to get to you, Hill, but it was too late."

"Sure, I heard. Thanks for trying anyways, *amigo*."

"This's my town, Hill," Dusty said quietly. "And I'm sworn in as a deputy sheriff of Edwards County."

No comments came from the two middle-aged outlaws, and Dusty expected none. Their kind lacked the intelligence to organise, or the ability to lead. Recognising their failings, they were content to take orders from a smarter man. Not so Joey. Young, ambitious, regarding himself as uncurried below the knees, he sought for ways to prove it.

"So?" he asked truculently.

"So I'll stop anything that starts, no matter who starts it and help run down anybody I have to," Dusty replied.

"You!" Joey spat out, shoving back his chair and reaching gun-wards as he started to rise. "Why you short-growed r—."

Swiftly Dusty estimated Joey's potential and decided on how to handle him. Fresh to the outlaw life, with a head full of ideas about his own toughness, the young man lacked experience. That showed in the way he acted. No man who knew the score would have taken such a chance when dealing with the almost legendary Rio Hondo gun wizard.

Before Joey could complete rising or draw his gun, Dusty

backhanded him savagely. Caught with the full force of a swing from a real powerful arm, Joey pitched backwards. His chair disintegrated under him and he sprawled heavily to the floor. Even so he still retained a grip of his gun and, despite being winded by the landing, jerked it from leather. Going around the table in a bound, Dusty sprang forward to lash out his foot. A howl of pain broke from Joey as the toe of Dusty's boot connected with his hand, sending the gun spinning from it. Bending down, Dusty laid hold of Joey's vest and almost ripped it from him while jerking the youngster erect.

"Sit fast!" Thompson ordered his men. "Maybe the kid'll get some sense knocked into his fool head."

Slamming the dazed youngster on his feet, Dusty released him. As Joey began to stagger, the small Texan smashed a punch into his belly. Up whipped Dusty's other hand, colliding with Joey's jaw as he folded over from the other blow. The youngster straightened once more, spun around and landed limply on the floor. Turning fast, Dusty faced the table with hands held ready to deal with any kind of attack. One glance told him that the rest of the party did not intend taking up the play for their companion.

"Keep him out of my way, Hill," he warned.

"Sure, Dusty. You boys take him out and wake him up, then make sure he doesn't come back."

"Sure, boss," replied one of the men. "Will you be needing us?"

"If I do, I'll shout," Thompson promised and watched his orders obeyed. Then he turned back to Dusty and grinned, "See you're as fast as ever."

"When I have to be," Dusty agreed.

At that moment a very nervous-looking Lily made her appearance. Coming across to the table, she prepared to make excuses and wondered how Dusty would regard finding outlaws in her place.

"The lady didn't know who we are, Dusty," Thompson stated, before she could speak. "I don't reckon she goes to her visitors and asks for references."

"She'd not have much trade if she did," Dusty replied. "That chair'll have to be paid for, Hill."

"I'll see to it," the outlaw promised.

"And I'd like to talk to him in private, Miss Lily," Dusty went on.

"My office's as private as you can get around here, Cap'n," Lily answered.

"Let's go, Hill," Dusty ordered.

"Like you said. It's your town."

Going into the madam's office, the two Texans sat at her desk. After offering to supply free drinks or food, Lily withdrew. At the door she paused, then, unable to decide what to do next, went out. Her bouncer came over and asked for orders.

"Go get some rest for tonight," she replied. "I figure the marshal knows what he's doing and don't need any help to do it."

"How's it going, Hill?" Dusty asked as the door closed behind Lily.

"I can't complain."

"Why not give yourself up? Davis' carpetbaggers aren't in office any more, so you'll get a fair trial."

"And go to jail for maybe ten or more years," Thompson answered. "I'd sooner live and die an owlhoot, Dusty."

"Then don't try anything in Mulrooney, or Edwards County," Dusty warned. "Like I said, I'll stop you if I have to. So don't make me do it."

"I didn't know who held the badge here," Thompson assured him. "And, as far as I know, I'm not up here to pull anything local."

"You don't know why you're here?"

"That's the living truth. All I heard was that Tricky Dick Cansole wanted for me to come up here to meet him."

"Cansole, huh?" Dusty repeated.

"Yeah," Thompson agreed. "You've likely heard of him, wearing a badge in a Kansas town, although he's not too well known in Texas. He passed word to me that he'd got something big coming up and needed extra help. Offered me five hundred just to come up and talk it over. I heard tell he's sent for Dick Dublin and Alf Marlow to come up. Word has it that he's calling down some north country hands as well."

"He must have something big on."

"Big enough to offer waiting money for them who stick around until he needs 'em," Thompson answered. "At least that's the word that came with the five hundred."

136

"You figuring on taking him up on whatever it is?" Dusty asked.

"I don't know until I've learned what the play is. Anyways, I reckon I'll take some waiting money for a spell. Texas's a mite too lively since the Rangers were brought back. You and your Hooded Riders sure spoiled things back to home, Dusty. If it hadn't been for them, we'd still only have the State Police to worry about. Which wasn't any worry at all."

A faint frown came to Dusty's face at the words. Despite the fact that he had played an important part in bringing a decent, elected government back to Texas, he still hated to be reminded of how it came about. Learning of a plot, hatched by certain members of the corrupt Davis administration, to ruin Texas' economy by wrecking the State's major industry, ranching, Dusty knew he must fight back. Yet to be caught, or even recognised, doing so would compromise his Uncle Ole Devil and other influential Texans who were working to regain the franchise for the people of the State. So, reluctantly, Dusty and the rest of the floating outfit had organised the Hooded Riders as a means of fighting the State Police. To a pure-dyed Texas fighting man like Dusty hiding his identity under a hood held no appeal. However he did so, achieved his goal, then tried to forget the means employed to do it.*

Then a thought struck him and he looked hard at Thompson. "How'd you know I ran them, Hill?"

"It wasn't hard. Those Hooded Riders worked like you did with Company 'C' in the War, fast and unexpected. Who else could it've been?"

"I hoped nobody knew," Dusty said quietly.

"Nobody does know, for sure. You must've had some mighty slick help to keep you so well informed about what the Yankees aimed to do next."

"You might say that."

"Anybody I'd know?"

"That's one thing I don't aim to tell," Dusty stated flatly.

With the War over, Belle Boyd had accepted an offer to join the Yankee Secret Service. One of her contacts had gained the information which led to the forming of the Hooded Riders and she passed on much news they used. The future safety of the

Told in THE HOODED RIDERS.

Rebel Spy depended too much on secrecy for Dusty to mention her part in the affair.

Not wishing for further discussion of what he regarded as a tasteless, unpleasant, if necessary, business, Dusty changed the subject.

"I'll only be here for another couple of weeks, Hill. Until Kale Beauregard comes up from the Indian Nations to take over. Don't pull anything while I'm here. I'd hate like hell to have to bring you in."

"But you'd do it," Thompson said, more as a statement than a question.

"I took an oath with the badge and I'll not break it."

"Which same I'd hate to put you where you might have to," Thompson said. "So me 'n' the boys'll ride back to the hideout and let Tricky come there to us." He grinned. "Don't suppose it's any use asking who told you I was here?"

"You're right," Dusty agreed. "It's not. *Adios*, Hill."

"*Hasta la vista*," Thompson replied. "Only not up here."

Just as Dusty prepared to leave, a thought struck him. "Say, Hill, how'd you know to meet Cansole in Mulrooney?"

"He sent word to the hideout for us to come up here instead of waiting for him," Thompson answered. "Said for us to stop at the house and he'd be in touch with us afore night."

Knowing that he would learn no more, and in fact knew more than he had a right to expect even from an old friend like Thompson, Dusty walked out of the house. Moving away without a backwards glance, Dusty thought over what Thompson told him. As he entered the trees, he saw Mark Counter leaning against the trunk of a large flowering dogwood.

"What the—!" Dusty began wrathfully.

"Sarah and Frank come in just after you left and allowed to want to be alone. So I thought I'd take a walk, not wanting to get the name for being a spoil-sport," Mark replied. "I just happened to be passing and leaned on the tree to rest my poor aching shoulder."

"I believe in fairies," Dusty growled. "Damn it, Mark. I said that I'd come here alone—."

"That's what you said," Mark interrupted. "Only who'd it be who had to go home to tell Ole Devil and Betty happen you got shot? Me, that's who."

"You've got a right smart point there," Dusty said in a milder

tone, his anger tempered by the knowledge that Mark's dis-
obedience stemmed from concern over his safety and well-being.
"If that shoulder's better now, we'll find some place where we
can keep watch from."

"Are you expecting trouble?"

"Nope. Just wanting to see who comes calling."

"Was it Hill Thompson there?" Mark inquired as they found
a place which allowed them to see front and rear of the house.

"Sure. He'll be pulling out soon."

"Did he say why he's here?"

"Tricky Dick Cansole sent for him."

A low whistle broke from Mark's lips and he asked, "Why?"

"To help pull something big," Dusty replied. "You know that
we've been wondering why Cansole tried to get Smith out; or if
he'd try again after losing those two men?"

"Sure," Mark agreed. "I'm starting to think that he's forgot
Smith and's set to take a loss on the hidden money."

"I'd've gone along with you this morning," Dusty admitted.
"Only now I reckon he's got to free Smith and lay hands on it."

"What'd Hill tell you?" Mark asked, guessing the source of
Dusty's changed opinion.

"That Cansole's calling in a slew of high-price help for whatever he plans. And offering to pay them to stick around until
the right time for it. That'd run into big money."

"Which he can't raise from more hold-ups after losing Stayley
and that other pair," Mark mused. "Say, if Hill came here,
Cansole must be in town or close by."

"That's why we're waiting," Dusty answered. "Even if it's
not Cansole who comes to meet Hill, whoever it is might lead us
to him."

Settling down with the patience acquired performing more
than one such task, the two Texans waited and watched. After
about half an hour Thompson and his men left, Joey supported
by the other two and offering no objections to the departure.
Time dragged by with no callers arriving. A couple of girls
emerged, passing the hidden lawmen and returned later carrying baskets of laundry. In another town Dusty might have suspected them, but he figured Lily had too much to lose to chance
siding with outlaws.

On their return to the office, the Kid and Waco listened as
Pickle-Barrel told what he—with Dusty's unspoken consent—

had overheard during the interview with the informer. Guessing what must have happened, the Kid told the others that he would go and lend a hand. Although Waco wanted to go along, the Kid stated his turn would come later.

When the Kid joined them, Dusty told Mark to return to the office, pay the informer another ten dollars and order him out of town. In case of objections, Mark was to hint that Smokey Hill Thompson might like to know who told Dusty of his presence. On hearing that, the informer left in a hurry and did not return.

At sundown Waco joined the watchers, sent by Mark to relieve Dusty. However by that time the evening's business had started to build up. Dusty decided that the man they wanted would not come. Or if he did, they had no way of knowing him. Figuring there would be plenty of other work to do, Dusty called off the surveillance and walked with his companions back towards the main business section of the town.

Passing the Fair Lady, Dusty glanced through the window. What he saw brought him to a halt. At his side Waco and the Kid also stopped and stared. While they all realised that the staff of the saloon regarded the feud with the Buffalo as a deadly serious affair, none expected it to be carried to such extremes.

The girl who first caught Dusty's eye wore a skirt that trailed to the floor—at the back. In front the material ended at the waist and was cut down almost to the nipples of her unsupported bosom. Although the Kid and Waco looked in frank approval, Dusty clearly found the sight less pleasing.

"Damn it!" he growled. "What in hell's Freddie reckon she's doing?"

Much as the Kid appreciated the female form so attractively displayed, he knew what Dusty meant. "Let's go look at what the Buffalo gals're wearing," he said.

On arrival, they found that Kate offered girls in outfits little more than bodices; ending at the level of frilly, brief drawers and with only one layer of cloth above the waist.

"I'll be damned if I'll ever credit a woman again with having good sense!" Dusty barked, stamping off along the sidewalk.

"What's riling him?" Waco asked. "Those gals look mighty good to me."

"And to them," the Kid replied, nodding to a group of goggle-eyed cowhands who came from the direction of the Fair Lady.

"There'll be trouble tonight, boy."

Before half past eight that evening Waco knew what riled Dusty and understood the Kid's cryptic utterance. By then they had quelled a near riot between gandy-dancers and the Buffalo's male staff, stopped a buffalo hunter attempting to drag a townswoman into a dark alley and prevented three cowhands chasing girls along the street.

At which point Dusty decided to put an end to one aspect of the feud. Sending for Freddie and Kate, he interviewed them in private. For the first time since they met Freddie was not treated as a lady and received a tongue-lashing she never forgot. Finally Dusty delivered an ultimatum: each saloon must get its girls back into suitable clothing before half an hour passed, or be closed down. Realising they had asked for all they received, and probably more, the women obeyed. However Dusty knew that the feud had not ended, nor would until they knew who was boss between them.

16

He Walked Right By Us into Town

The full story of how the rivalry between Freddie Woods and Buffalo Kate Gilgore came to its explosive head has been told elsewhere.* Briefly, a group of prominent Brownton citizens, finding their town did not render the expected financial success hoped for, planned to use the feud as a means to help them rob the Mulrooney bank. In addition to offering them a better than fair profit, it would also ruin the other town. By a trick the Brownton crowd brought Freddie and Kate together in a boxing ring, relying on the noisy approval of the audience to drown the noise as they blew the safe. This failed due to Wally and Vera, acting as seconds to their respective employers, drugging both contestants in an attempt to keep them from inflicting too much damage on each other. The collapse of Freddie and Kate came just as the explosion sounded, and the lawmen heard it in

*Told in THE TROUBLE BUSTERS.

the shocked hush following the abrupt end of the fight.

Although Dusty feared the fight might be a trick on Cansole's part, he took all the deputies to the Buffalo Saloon; leaving Pickle-Barrel locked in the jail with orders not to open up to anybody but himself. So he had the means on hand to break up the hold-up, although the task of halting the riot which started among the disappointed and angry crowd fell upon Big Sarah.

Learning the identity of the robbery's organisers from one of the men who attempted it and was captured, Dusty received a warrant for their arrest. Although it was then Sunday, he intended to head for Brownton and serve it. Then word came that Kate meant to force a showdown with Freddie that morning. Once again Dusty faced a problem of what to do. At last he decided that the Brownton bunch must be brought in. Sarah claimed she could confine the trouble between Freddie and Kate to the Fair Lady, so once more Pickle-Barrel received his orders to remain in the locked building and admit nobody. While Dusty and the male deputies rode out, the female staff of the two saloons came together in a clash which finally brought an end to the feud.

In the middle of the afternoon Dusty's party returned. As they approached Mulrooney, bringing two wounded Brownton citizens in a buggy, they saw a couple of rifle-armed riders galloping their way.

"What's up?" Dusty asked, recognising the men as a gandy-dancer and cowhand who had each spent a night in the jail for being drunk on the streets.

"There's been trouble down at the pokey, Cap'n," the cowhand replied. "M—!"

Dusty waited to hear no more. Setting his spurs to the huge paint, he sent it racing towards the town. Leaving Derringer to continue driving the buggy and bring in its occupants, only one of whom was a prisoner, the floating outfit went hot-foot after their leader.

Ignoring the men gathered before the office, although they came from every section of the community and visitors, Dusty brought his paint to a halt. He hit the ground before the huge animal stopped, leaving it free as he crossed the sidewalk to enter the building. Inside he found two trail bosses, the head of the railroad division based on Mulrooney and a pair of prominent buffalo hunters. Slumped in a chair, dressed in her town

142

clothes, cleaned up but showing signs of what had been one hell of a fight, Freddie raised a face lined with remorse and anxiety to look at the new arrival.

"What happened?" Dusty asked, speaking to Sarah who stood at Freddie's side.

"It was near on noon when I got here, what with one thing and another," the big female deputy answered in a husky, grief-ladened voice. "I found Pickles—dead on the floor and Smith gone."

"God damn it!" Dusty blazed, swinging in sudden fury to face Freddie. "If you and Kate hadn't—."

"You don't have to tell me about that," Freddie answered in a sick voice.

Not since the day outside Dodge City, when Bat Masterson told Dusty that the wrangler of the Rocking H trail herd had been killed in mistake for him, had Mark and the Kid seen him so angry.* Freddie sank into herself and seemed almost on the verge of tears, all her calm self-possession gone before his fury. It was Big Sarah who spoke first.

"Leave her be, Cap'n. Miss Freddie's near on crazy with sorrowing now. Only as soon as she heard what'd happened, hurt like she is, she come down here to do what she could. And she's done plenty."

"That's true, Captain Fog," the railroad supervisor went on. "Freddie's got every trail crew's scout cutting for sign around town, had groups of men searching every empty house, or unoccupied place in town. Few men could have organised things better."

"You've no call to rawhide her, Cap'n," one of the buffalo-hunters went on.

"When I want you t—!" Dusty began; then the others could see him make a visible effort to control his temper. "You're right, friend. I'm sorry, Freddie."

"It *was* all my fault," Freddie replied and extended her arms. "Lord! I'd have cut my hands off at the wrists rather than have—."

"It's done with, Freddie," Dusty said in a gentle tone. Then he became cold and business-like. "How'd they get in, Sarah?"

"Now there you've got me, Cap'n," she replied, putting aside her annoyance at him for his treatment of Freddie. "The place

*Told in TRAIL BOSS.

143

was locked up tight when I came down. I used the key you gave me to get in."

"Unless you took it with you, they went out of the back door, locked it from the outside and took the key along," Freddie put in. "I checked on it."

"Thanks, Freddie. Did you—How long'd Pickles been dead when you found him, Sarah?"

"Not long," the woman replied and her face showed emotion. "He was still warm when I—I—."

"You did good," Dusty assured her quietly. "Only don't go woman on me now."

"He couldn't've been dead for more than half an hour," Sarah stated. "I wasn't sure what to do, so I headed for the Fair Lady and told Miss Freddie. She did the rest."

Which, if her present condition meant anything, must have put her through hell. However Dusty held back his comments and thoughts of gratitude until a more suitable time. At that moment his sole concern was to learn all he could.

"No fresh hoss or any other kind of tracks leaving town, Dusty," one of the trail bosses announced. "And I sent men on speed-hosses along every trail to see if they could learn anything. I'd swear they never left town by hoss or wagon."

"There've been neither stage nor trains leave," the supervisor went on. "So they must be here someplace."

"Not in any empty place, we've looked in 'em all," stated the buffalo-hunter. "Which means, unless they've done gone off in one of them balloons the Yankees used in the War, they must be hid in town."

While listening to every word said, Waco could not help noticing the way the different factions of the town worked together and how they gave Dusty their willing co-operation. Faced with a crisis, the careful, fair, honest effort put into enforcing the law in Mulrooney had paid off. Few other trail-end town marshals holding office in Kansas could have claimed such a response.

After thinking on that for a moment, Waco turned his attention to other, more important issues. Ever since Freddie held out her soft, well-cared for hands, something had gnawed at the youngster. Then memory flooded back.

"And I reckon I know where they're hid out," the youngster

144

said, wishing only the other members of the office stood listening.

"Where?" Dusty demanded.

"It's only a guess, mind. But I reckon they're at that convent."

"Go on, boy," Dusty encouraged.

"There's something about that new mother superior never rode right with me, Dusty," Waco continued. "Now I know what it was."

"What?"

"It's her hands. Soft, white, with long nails, like she'd never done a lick of work in her life. All the other nuns work too hard to have hands like that—or the ones I saw around the place did—."

"A nun, even a mother superior, with soft white hands and long nails would be unusual," Freddie remarked.

"And she sure wears fancy shoes," the youngster went on, grateful for the confirmation. "I got a peek at 'em as she crossed the railer—Hell's fire! That nun with her must've been Tricky Dick Cansole. He walked right by us into town!"

"You're making good sense," Dusty told him.

"There's another thing," Waco replied. "When I was fetching them two nesters in I met her, the mother superior, out back there. She allowed to be going to see some sick folks. If it'd've been anybody but a nun, I'd've fetched 'em in to tell you about it. But it being her, I took her word. She could've been talking to Smith. The morning after he started to perk up again instead of acting a mite edgy and worried."

"Ole Pickles wouldn't've opened up to anybody—," the Kid growled. "Except somebody like a nun."

"Just like the Bad Bunch!" Mark breathed.

"Just like it," Dusty agreed, thinking back to the notorious gang which had plagued Texas, and brought him and Mark close to death before being broken up.* "And likely they're still hid out in the convent, waiting for the hunt to die off."

"Oh my god!" Freddie suddenly gasped, stiffening in her chair. "The convent—!"

"What's wrong with it?" Dusty asked.

"Every Sunday since it opened I've sent two baskets of food around, some delicacies they wouldn't have otherwise—."

"So?"

*Told in THE BAD BUNCH.

"So Babsy took them today. Ginger went along, I think to prove that she was as tough as Babsy—."

"Babsy!" Waco spat out and started to turn. "Then she might be—."

Dusty caught his hand in a tight, firm grip. "Hold hard there, boy. We don't know there's anything wrong."

"Dammit, she might be—."

"And if she is, one sight of you charging out there waving your guns could see her dead, or used as a hostage, which'd wind up the same."

Despite his concern for the little girl's safety, Waco realised that Dusty spoke the truth. He saw that his original plan—or intention, for no planned thought prompted his actions—would not do.

"We've got to do something!" the youngster insisted.

"And we'll make a start at doing it right now," Dusty answered. "Lon, get over to the convent, only don't let them know you're watching it—."

"Let me go," Waco requested.

"I want you with me," Dusty replied.

"Don't you trust me?"

"If I didn't, you'd not've started to wear that badge. I want you to go in there with me when the right time comes."

Even discounting the youngster's personal stake in the affair, Dusty knew him to be the best choice. With Mark still unable to make full use of his left hand, Waco stood next in revolver-shooting ability. Up close, as they must be inside the building, a handgun licked a rifle even in the Kid's highly-skilled grip.

"Sure, Dusty," Waco said contritely. "Times I talk too much."

"If it wasn't for the company you keep, I'd say you'd grow out of it," Dusty answered. "Sarah, head for the Fair Lady and see if the gals're back."

"Yo!" she replied, dropping into the old cavalry assent almost automatically. Then she and the Kid left the room.

"Get some of those fellers to help Frank Derringer, Gil," Dusty said to one of the trail bosses as the buggy halted outside.

"It's done," came the reply and the man went to obey.

"What do we do, Dusty?" asked Waco.

"Just about the hardest thing, boy—Wait."

Any slight hope the party held for the two girls' safety died when Sarah returned with word that they had not come back to the Fair Lady.

"What now, Dusty?" asked the railroad supervisor. "Do we smoke 'em out?"

"Only by doing it my way," the small Texan replied. "I want every man you can lay hands on strung around town so tight that a gopher couldn't crawl through even in the dark. Only keep them out of sight of the convent. Mark'll show you where to go."

"Let's make a start," Mark ordered.

"If that's all you want—," the supervisor replied.

"The rest's up to us," Dusty told him. "Make sure those fellers know not to come closer, Mark."

Leaving the office, Mark started the organisation. While the supervisor had expected objections from the gandy-dancers to taking orders from a deputy who was also a cowhand, none came. O'Sullivan, Voigt and Rastignac collectively promised to half-kill any railroad man who failed to obey; and their threats carried weight.

"This's how I figure we'll play it," Dusty told Waco, Freddie and Sarah, Derringer being occupied with the Brownton prisoner.

"I'm the one to help you, Dusty," Freddie stated after hearing the plan. "It's my fault this happ—."

"Which doesn't worry me right now," Dusty interrupted. "I'm taking you because I reckon you can handle it best. Can you get what you'll need?"

"Easily," she assured him. "How about you?"

"We've got all but one thing. Moccasins, our guns."

"What else do you need?" Freddie inquired.

"Lon's knife," Dusty replied and something in his voice made her shudder. "Clean your guns, boy."

"But—."

"We can't move until after dark—And you can't chance having a misfire through not taking care of your Colts," Dusty said quietly. "Get to it, and I'll do mine."

Hearing a knocking at the front door, Tricky Dick Cansole and Stella Castle looked at each other. The outlaw fitted Sheriff Bracker's description, being stylishly dressed, medium-sized and almost effeminate in appearance. However the two Webley

147

Bulldog revolvers thrust into his waist band were deadly weapons in his long-fingered hands.

"I'll see who it is and get rid of them," Stella promised, adjusting her nun's headdress. "And you three stay in here with the door closed. If that fool Triblet hadn't been wandering around, we wouldn't have this pair of calico cats on our hands."

They stood in the large room which would be the chapel, although as yet it was uncompleted. Behind them, roped to chairs and gagged, sat Babsy, Ginger, each sporting signs of their fight, and Sister Bridget. Smith came to join Cansole and Stella while the tall, gaunt owlhoot named Triblet turned from the window where he had been watching the land behind the building.

"Go to it," Cansole ordered. "Nobody suspects that we're here."

On stepping into the entrance hall, Stella saw Sister Teresa emerge from the lower floor room where the nuns had been ordered to stay.

"You make one sound, or fancy move, and they'll kill Sister Bridget," Stella hissed, wondering how the girl had got out of the locked room.

Before taking the veil, Sister Teresa had been a criminal and had learned to pick locks from her father. While she had failed to open the nailed-to shutters at the window, she had dealt with the lock, but too slowly to reach the door and give a warning. Stella thought of ordering the girl back into the room, but decided Sister Teresa admired the big Irish nun too much to endanger her life. Having the girl in plain sight would serve to hold down any suspicions should it be men searching for the escaped prisoner.

Going along to the front door, Stella darted a glance behind her. Sister Teresa stood silent, watching, but the door to the chapel remained closed. Then Stella looked through the window beside the door. Despite her belief that nobody suspected anything, she felt just a twinge of concern at seeing law badges reflected in the light of the lamp outside.

Standing just outside, the marshal and that damned blond kid supported a dancehall girl who appeared to be in pain. Dressed in the garish clothing of her kind, black hair untidy and bare shoulders mottled with bruises, she hung in their arms, head drooping and body sagging as she held her ribs with her hands. Behind them stood the woman deputy. As Stella opened the door, she heard the end of a conversation specially carried out for her benefit.

"Damn this slut!" Dusty was growling. "I should be out on the range with a posse, not foo—Howdy, ma'am."

"What is it?" Stella inquired, holding down a smile at the change in tone.

"This cali—gal got hurt in the fight this morning," Dusty replied and Freddie accompanied the words with a sobbing moan that sounded genuine. "It was worse than they figured and she needs caring for."

"But the doctor—."

"He's had to go out to a farm, ma'am. And seeing's how this gal's one of your folk, I reckoned you'd tend to her."

"She was asking to come here and won't rest easy any other place," Sarah put in.

"But I—We aren't a nursing order," Stella said hesitantly, unsure of just what kind of order the nuns might be. "Surely—."

"Folks'll reckon it's mighty un-Christian happen you turn her away, ma'am," Dusty remarked.

True enough, but far worse to Stella's way of thinking was that a refusal might arouse the small Texan's suspicions. From what Triblet told them, Dusty Fog packed considerable savvy at his work and could not be underestimated in the thinking line. Already he had caused every building which did not have occupants searched, even before Smith's rescue, so he must suspect their presence in town. Give him reason to doubt her *bona fides* and she did not doubt that Dusty would come up with the right answers.

"If you don't want the fellers inside, I'll help you tote her," Sarah offered, darting a glance at Sister Teresa who was hovering in the background.

"It may be best," Stella agreed. "Once she's in, we can manage her."

From the look and sound of the 'injured' Freddie, Stella did not doubt she could prevent the other raising any outcry on learning the true state of affairs. So she stepped outside, doing what Dusty gambled she would. He saw the other occupant of the hall was a woman, guessed she did not belong to the gang and figured Stella had her there to quiet any suspicions, relying on the vow of silence or threats to keep her quiet.

Just an instant too late Stella realised her mistake. Even before she reached the trio, the men released the woman. Opening her mouth to scream a warning, Stella tried to halt her forward progress. Like a flash Freddie moved, ripping her clenched fist with all her power full into the pit of the other woman's stomach. Stella's scream finished before it started as agony knotted her body and the breath burst from her lungs.

Moving fast, Dusty shot out his hand, caught Stella and prevented her from stumbling back into the hall. With a surging heave he swung her around and backed her into the wall. Holding her erect with one hand, he reached out to take the Kid's bowie knife—borrowed on their arrival—from Sarah who had kept it concealed until the appropriate moment.

"Make one lil sound and I'll mark you so bad you'll never dare face folk again!" he snarled, holding the knife's razor sharp blade close to Stella's face.

Probably no other threat could have ensured the woman's complete silence. Hurt and winded though she might be, without the menace to her beautiful features she would have chanced giving the warning and relied on Cansole to save her. Yet she believed that Dusty aimed to do what he said and so stood as if frozen.

"Let me have her, Cap'n," Sarah said.

"Sure," Dusty answered and waited until the big woman took hold before releasing her. "Let's go, boy."

Without speaking Sister Teresa pointed out the door behind which Cansole held the hostages, then she stood watching the Texans approach it on silent feet.

Holding their guns, Dusty and Waco halted on either side of the door. Quietly Dusty stepped around in front of it, satisfied the men inside did not know they were there. Then he braced himself ready to perform a technique learned from Tommy Okasi. While Dusty could not equal his teacher's *tameshiwari* ability in breaking wood or stone with the bare hands and feet, he felt adequate for the work to hand.

Inhaling deeply through the nose, Dusty composed himself for the effort. A glance at Waco told him the youngster stood waiting. So Dusty gave the traditional spiritual cry of "Kiai!" and drove his right foot with all his power into the door. As it burst inwards, Waco plunged through, going across to the left. A moment later Dusty entered the chapel headed the other way.

150

For once Tricky Dick Cansole had been over-confident. Satisfied that the local law did not know of his presence in town, he had taken no other precautions than preventing the three prisoners from making any noise. While Cansole held one of his Webleys, he did not line it at Babsy although standing at her side. Gripping a Colt, Triblet held it to Sister Bridget's head. Smith contented himself with using his good hand to cover Ginger's gagged mouth.

When the door burst open Cansole and Triblet swung their weapons towards it and Smith belatedly started to draw. However the way the Texans entered threw the outlaws off balance. Fast as a striking diamondback, Cansole fired at Dusty but missed. Almost as swiftly Triblet threw down on Waco while the youngster prepared to shoot Cansole, the menacer of Babsy.

Unlike Waco and Dusty—due to the small Texan's forethought —Triblet did not take trouble to care for his gun. Its hammer fell on a percussion cap so long on the nipple as to become inoperative. Only a click sounded. Before Triblet could recock the gun, Dusty drove a bullet into his head.

Showing the same speed as when shooting, Cansole hurled himself backwards. He missed death by inches as Waco's bullet fanned by his head. Recognising the quality of the opposition, Cansole knew better than make a fight. Twisting around, he raced across the room and dived head-first through the window before Waco had a chance to fire again. Already having tasted the Texans' deadly brand of gun-play, Smith jerked his hand away from the weapon and yelled that he gave up.

"He's mine, Dusty!" Waco yelled, running across the room. Yet even at such a moment he remembered to take a basic precaution. "Lon! Don't shoot. I'm coming out!"

And, warning the Kid that a friend would be the next to appear, the youngster sprang into the darkness to give chase to the fleeing Tricky Dick Cansole.

17

That was Real Smart Advice

When Cansole burst through the window, the Kid snapped off a quick shot. In the poor light the deadly Winchester missed, although not by much. The bullet passed the outlaw close enough to hand him a nasty shock, but only caused him to run the faster. Before the Kid could take sight again, he heard Waco's shout, saw the youngster follow Cansole out of the building and held his fire. Nor did he follow as Waco gave chase to the fleeing Cansole. A skilled night-fighter, the Kid knew his presence would be a liability to Waco. The youngster stood a better chance alone and free from the danger of shooting at a friend instead of the enemy.

Thinking back to a comment made by himself earlier, the Kid grinned. "Yes sir," he thought, walking towards the convent. "*This's* sure one place that won't cause us any trouble."

Racing along, Cansole looked back over his shoulder. From the speed the young deputy followed, he wore something more suitable for running than the usual high-heeled cowhand boots. So he must be killed if the outlaw hoped to escape. The problem being how to bring this off without taking a .44 Colt bullet in return.

Suddenly Cansole skidded to a turning halt, threw up his right hand Webley and fired. At the same moment Waco swerved, ducked down and flame licked out from his Colt. Cansole's bullet missed and he heard the sound of Waco's lead passing his head. Fast taken, while on the move, the youngster's bullet failed to connect by such a narrow margin that it served as a grim warning. It confirmed Cansole's judgement of his ability. The outlaw knew that he must take no chances when dealing with so efficient a gun-fighter. However trickery might prevail where skill failed.

Close by stood an empty house and Cansole headed towards it. Finding the door unfastened, he jerked it open. Turning, he threw another shot in Waco's direction. Then he entered the building, closed the door behind him and backed off across the room. Halting at the opposite wall, he glanced at the square of the unfinished window. The sound of approaching feet jerked his attention back to the door. Hearing the sound of the deputy trying the handle, he fired three shots, angling them to fan across the entrance. An agony-filled cry rang out from beyond the door, followed by the thud of a falling body. Satisfied that he had dealt with the deputy, Cansole walked across to the window and kicked aside a plank blocking his way through it. Once outside, providing no other lawmen were close at hand, he could make his way into town, steal a horse and escape.

Following Cansole, Waco approached the door with the intention of crashing through it. Then he remembered what Dusty told him and slowed down, stepping silently to the left. From there he reached around, gripping the handle as if meaning to thrust the door open.

"That was real smart advice, Dusty," he breathed as the bullets burst outwards throwing splinters before them. If he had been stood in the normal position to open the door, one or more of them would have torn into his body.

Only the youngster did not waste time in idle self-congratulation. Letting out a screech like a man caught by a bullet, he flung himself backwards and lit down with a thud. That ought to convince Cansole there was no further danger, the youngster assumed and braced himself ready to charge into the building. The sound of the knocked-aside plank reached his ears and he darted along the front of the building and turned the corner. Ahead of him Cansole had already climbed through the window.

"Cansole!" Waco yelled, sliding to a halt.

The outlaw turned fast, gun bellowing as he came around. However he moved too fast. Waco felt as if a hot iron sliced over his ribs, but did not let it prevent him cutting loose with both Colts, having drawn the left hand gun while rounding the building. Left, right, left, right, the long-barrelled Army Colts spat. Caught by the bullets, Cansole reeled and hurtled backwards. The Webleys dropped from his hands as he crashed to the ground. Any one of the four bullets would have killed him.

"You all right, boy?" came the Kid's voice.

"He nicked me, but I'm still on my feet," Waco called back.

Coming up, the Kid looked anxiously at Waco, then to where Cansole lay unmoving on the ground.

"You've done good. Go tell Dusty what's happened. I reckon I can tend to him now."

"Yeah," Waco replied and managed a faint grin. "I reckon you can."

An hour later, the graze on his ribs stitched up and bandaged, Waco sat in the marshal's office with the other deputies and listened to Stella Castle talk. Thoroughly scared and wanting to save her neck, the woman insisted on making a full confession.

On hearing of Smith's capture, Cansole guessed that his orders regarding the loot had been carried out. Needing the money to pay the outlaws gathered for his big scheme, Cansole knew he must try to rescue the prisoner. When the first try failed, he decided to handle the affair himself, particularly in the face of his men's opposition to making the next attempt.

Although Stella insisted she did not know where Cansole had obtained the nuns' clothing, Dusty believed she lied. It would never be proved that the man murdered the original mother superior and a novice. Their bodies, buried outside Newton, were never found.

On arrival in Mulrooney, they went to the convent and took its occupants prisoner before being suspected. Using the well-liked Sister Bridget as a hostage, they prevented the other nuns from trying to escape and managed to keep up appearances by having a few of them working outside. Triblet came in to town on the buggy of a contact, hiding at the convent except when needed to meet somebody. It had been him who should have met Hill Thompson, but saw the outlaws leaving, smelled a rat and kept away from the brothel.

Fearing that Smith might feel neglected, Stella visited him and passed word through the bars of his cell window that Cansole was in town, preparing to free him. She directed a venomous glare at Waco while commenting on the scare he gave her.

Due to various reasons, Cansole failed to take advantage of the Saturday night diversion created by the Brownton men. Instead of telling his boss about the proposed fight, Triblet stayed at the Buffalo Saloon to watch, then became involved in the after-fight riot. By the time he returned to the convent, it was too late for them to make a move.

That morning when Triblet brought word that Dusty and the male deputies were out of town, with Big Sarah fully occupied in supervising the brawl at the Fair Lady, Cansole saw his chance. Dressed as a nun, he gained access to the marshal's office and killed Pickle-Barrel, then freed Smith and brought him back to the convent. Although they planned to leave as soon as possible, Freddie's quick action prevented them from doing so. After seeing the searching of the empty buildings and noting that nobody gave the convent a second glance, Cansole decided to lie low there until an opportunity to escape presented itself.

While delivering the baskets of food, Babsy and Ginger saw Triblet in the building. So they had to be taken captive and held. The rest the listening men all knew.

"If that bastard Triblet had told us about Saturday!" she spat out. "Or come back earlier today instead of hanging around hoping to see those lousy bitches fighting—."

"Only he didn't," Dusty told her. "Put her in a cell, Sarah."

"Sister Bridget suggested that seeing's how she was all set at at looking like a nun, she ought to learn to act like one, Cap'n," the woman deputy replied. "You know, like digging the garden they've had to neglect, painting, scrubbing floors."

"Let her start in the morning," Dusty answered.

"It'll be a pleasure," Sarah grinned. "Come on, girlie and just give me one itsy-bitsy chance to stop you misbehaving."

"Smith's ready to talk, Dusty," Mark said as the women left the room.

"Leave the Wells Fargo boys to handle that part of it," Dusty replied. "I wonder what that big job was to be?"

"Reckon that gal didn't know?" asked the Kid, for Stella disclaimed all knowledge of it when questioned.

"I'm not sure," Dusty admitted. "Maybe after she's had Sister Bridget and Sarah looking to her for a spell, she'll change her mind."

The hope did not materialise. Whatever big robbery Cansole planned, his death prevented it happening.

"Sure is quiet and peaceful tonight," Mark commented, opening the front door. "I reckon I'll be getting to bed."

"I've got to go down and see Freddie," Dusty went on, for

155

the lady saloon-keeper had gone to the Fair Lady as soon as she knew Waco was all right.

Coming to his feet, Waco yawned as openly as he could. "Seeing's how I've done *all* the work tonight," he said. "I allow I can go off—Reckon you boys can manage without me?"

"We'll make sure you're close to hand," Derringer assured him.

Before the youngster could object, his friends descended on him, picked him up and carried him into the rear of the building. There they dumped him in an empty cell and locked him inside.

"Maybe comes morning you'll've learned to keep quiet," the Kid said.

"Anyways," Dusty went on. "Stopping to sleep in the cell's something else a lawman has to learn."

Left alone, the youngster settled on the bunk and grinned up at the roof. They were sure a great bunch of fellers to have for friends and they had taught him much of what it took to make a lawman.

Interested readers can read about the work of a present day sheriff's office in THE PROFESSIONAL KILLERS *by J. T. Edson, the first of his new series of Rockabye County stories. Mr. Edson will also continue to write new books about the adventures of Dusty Fog, Mark Counter, The Ysabel Kid, Waco and the others he has made famous.*

Other favourites from the Corgi Western range include:

Another action-packed Western by Louis L'Amour!

DARK CANYON

Dark Canyon was a tough stretch of bad country. Rustlers used it to drive stolen cattle. Desperate men skulked in it when they were in trouble. It was a road for bandit raids.

But Gaylord Riley didn't scare easy. He was lean-hipped and narrow-eyed, slick as lightning with a gun. He set up a cattle range bordering Dark Canyon. And when the men from the town of Rimrock rode out asking questions – Riley answered them – with a gun. So trouble came to Dark Canyon.

0 552 08173 6   25p

Another Louis Masterson book in the Morgan Kane series!

NO. 16 RETURN TO ACTION

Kane was enjoying a life of contented peace in the mountains of New Mexico with his pretty young wife, Linda. He made a living by catching and selling half-wild horses. It was a frugal existence, but a happy one – until the brutal gang of killers arrived at his home. They murdered Linda and stole six of Kane's horses. From that day Kane was a man with only one purpose in life: to avenge his wife's murder. With his two Mexican friends, Rico and Casca, he set out in pursuit of the gang . . .

0 552 08990 7   25p

From the 'Sudden' series by Oliver Strange:

SUDDEN RIDES AGAIN

He rode a horse as black as night. He wore two guns tied low, the butts worn smooth as the leather they nestled in. He was James Green: gunfighter, killer, murderer – a man with the kind of reputation that stilled hands on the way to holstered Colts.

He was an outlaw, heading for a deadly double-agent's game in an outpost of hell itself!

0 552 09064 6   22½p

A SELECTED LIST OF FINE NOVELS
from the
CORGI WESTERN RANGE

All these books are available at your bookshop or newsagent: or can be ordered direct from the publisher. Just tick the titles you want and fill in the form below.

....

CORGI BOOKS, Cash Sales Department, P.O. Box 11, Falmouth, Cornwall.
Please send cheque or postal order. No currency, and allow 6p per book to cover the cost of postage and packing in the U.K., and overseas.

NAME ....

ADDRESS ....

(JULY 73) ....